COL

The Dean's Death

is a Star original

TV's STAR SUPERCOPS

Coming soon

KOJAK:
Requiem for a Cop

KOJAK:
Girl in the River

KOJAK:
Siege

HAWAII FIVE-O:
The Angry Battalion

Plus a continuing series from COLUMBO and KOJAK, and a series introducing BBC TV's gourmet detective CANNON.

COLUMBO

The Dean's Death

Alfred Lawrence

Based on the Universal Television Series
COLUMBO
Created by RICHARD LEVINSON & WILLIAM LINK
Adapted from the episode 'By Dawn's Early Light'
Written by HOWARD BERK
Starring PETER FALK

A STAR BOOK
published by
W. H. ALLEN

A Star Book
Published in 1975
by W. H. Allen & Co. Ltd
A division of Howard & Wyndham Ltd
44, Hill Street, London W1X 8LB

Printed in Great Britain by
Richard Clay (The Chaucer Press), Ltd, Bungay, Suffolk

ISBN 0 352 30079 5

CHAPTER 1

Meredith College lies in neat green squares and orange stucco blocks of buildings across several acres of palm tree studded land near Los Angeles. Meredith is a medium-sized liberal arts college attempting to educate three thousand students a year, mostly in the arts, but the college does provide history, literature and language courses along with a small but excellent pre-med program.

With the exception of one New England style building, Meredith's architecture reflects the Spanish colonial stucco prevalent along Southern California freeways. This one building, of red brick and white wood trim, is Meredith Hall, the administration building, named for Martin 'Monk' Meredith, the founder of the college. The large structure was the eccentric millionaire's home, which he built to remind him of his New England boyhood, where he suffered poverty and humiliation before coming west and striking it rich in oil and real estate. Upon his death, Meredith, a man for whom no amount of money cleansed the embarrassment of a mediocre education, left his home and fortune to a board of distinguished trustees to convert into a University in his memory. The trustees, acting with some haste built dormitories, class buildings and a theater, all of which depleted the basic funding to a level where today Meredith's fortunes ride the see-saw of state funding, foundation grants and almost constant fund-raising drives. This is not to say the school has ever been strapped for money. It is just that caught between rising costs and dangerously fixed income the President of Meredith spends the majority of his time wooing politicians and hustling grants. How strange, then, to find the President of Meredith, Franklin Torrance smiling with satisfaction at a scolding letter from a major foundation rejecting the college's latest request for funds.

Yet, Torrance was unmistakably pleased and deeply satisfied by the refusal. It suited his plans perfectly.

The President of Meredith was a lean elegant man with dark hair neatly flecked with gray; he favored blue suits, colored shirts and contrasting ties. He looked more the Eastern University President than the Western. Walking into a room, he carried the cool self-assurance of New England patricianism: a shock to Southern Californians. He was self-secure and cautious in his actions and relationships; an apparently passionless man; one in full control of an intelligent mind, a large institution and his own life. A man whom you would swear could never be caught off guard.

His office was one of 'Monk' Meredith's bedrooms: redwood panels, chrystal chandelier, California sunshine sparkling through the high windows tinted pale blue. The windows overlooked an elegant formal garden. A light breeze disturbed the gauzy white curtains; blue and gold drapes were gathered into the corners. Portraits of three past Meredith Presidents hung on the walls. Two wing-backed chairs and matching sofa comprised a group around the fireplace. A thick, royal blue carpet added to the serenity and quiet of the chamber. Torrance's desk was pre-Revolutionary American maple.

*

The letter in front of Torrance was from Vincent Walter, President of the prestigious Vermeer Foundation, one of those barely known philanthropic organizations which specializes in parcelling out its hundreds of millions of dollars for extremely special projects, which few people ever hear about.

Walter was an old friend of Torrance's but in this letter he slapped his friend's hand for frivolity. 'Not the socially significant or innovative project we associate with Meredith College . . .' Torrance sighed deeply and smiled. He could salvage the grant any time. The important thing right now was to have it appear to be lost. As he was about to ring for his secretary, Miss Purdom, she rang him.

'Dean Borchardt wonders if you're free, Sir?'

'Ah, perfect,' thought President Torrance. 'Yes, all right,' he said aloud. No doubt the ugly little man wanted to discuss the grant refusal. The rejected plan, a school for Indian Studies, was one of Borchardt's pet ideas. It was an attempt at getting with the times, of placating the minority groups and the students whom Torrance thought were only pseudo-social activists. The Indian fad would pass with all the other movements of the last five years: blacks, peace, women's rights, chicanos . . . But indians were fashionable these days and it was Dean Borchardt's genius (now rebuffed by the foundation) to know just *what* social causes would command the most publicity at any given time.

And there he was, suddenly standing in front of Torrance: Arnold Borchardt, short and swarthy. No doubt he was a clean fellow, the President mused, but he had an absolute gift for looking slovenly. Borchardt wore neatly pressed black pants, some kind of comfortable suede walking shoe, a pale gray LaCoste sports shirt and a gray searsucker jacket. In spite of the cool colors, the immaculate pressing of each individual item, Arnold Borchardt looked like he'd just rolled in from a week riding cross-country on a Greyhound bus. Probably his heavy beard and those cold black eyes, Torrance thought. Men with heavy whiskers rarely look clean. The President suppressed a sneer.

'Yes, Arnold?'

'You saw the letter from the Vermeer Fund?'

'I read my mail.'

'It's a goddamn shame is what it is!'

'We can straighten it out.'

'If you don't we blow a million and a half—!'

'And your pet redskins. Calm down, man.'

'No need to condescend or sneer at indians.'

'I'm in a sneering mood this morning. I can't sneer at you – you're the dean of students. I'll sneer at some second-class citizens.'

'Very funny. But it's a damned good idea and I can't think why they turned it down.'

'Vince Walter doesn't owe me any more favors. He's paid me off for getting him the job at the Foundation with three consecutive grants. This one he thought was a safe bet for declaring his independence.'

'Every white man uses indian carcasses to declare his own independence!'

'I can't think of any other reason for turning us down.'

'I think I can, Frank.'

'And you're bursting to tell me about it.' Torrance smiled. He enjoyed baiting passionate men. They always rose to the lure. 'Tell me.'

'I read the proposal this morning. Twice. It wasn't at

all the way I'd written it initially. I think when you took it over to "improve it" you sabotaged it.'

Torrance uncrossed his legs folded his hands on his desk and leaned toward Borchardt. The chill in his voice would have put frost on the palm trees: '*Sit down!*'

'I'll stand, Frank.'

Torrance leaned back in his chair again. 'Stand then. You're doing the same thing you always do. You're hunting fleas with an elephant gun. I'll accept criticism. You might have said, "you diluted my original proposal" or "I wish you'd left this in my hands" but sabotage . . . dear, dear, Dean Borchardt, cash flow is my business. I'm not about to lose one single penny for this university. One-and-a-half million dollars is a bit much to play with.'

Borchardt sat down. 'All right! I'd given you a damn good proposal. Timely. Relevant and worthwhile. You made it look like another academic pork barrel with highly intellectual motives. Damn! I'm not after academic kudos for indian studies. I want to bring the best minds on the reservations in here to study. You made the whole thing sound like a research project. The Vermeer trustees turned it down because it sounded exploitative. Well it isn't. That's what I mean by sabotage.'

'I'll call Vince later and cajole him. He'll reopen the request.'

'No he won't.'

Torrance rose out of his chair. 'Is that right?'

'I talked to him five minutes ago. He said the presentation was the most inept he's ever had from you. That's why I said sabotage. I think you wanted me to look foolish. Everyone knows the Indian studies program is my pet. By engineering a foundation rejection you discredit me, not yourself.'

Torrance walked to the window. He stared at the softly swaying palm trees. He missed the oak and elms of his native New England. Borchardt was right. He was on to Torrance's game. Torrance could not stand the ill-kempt, ugly little man. It wasn't only the Dean's intellectual superiority that disgusted him, but the man's naked ambition. Borchardt was proving a deft academic politician, manoeuvering carefully to get ahead of Torrance in the race for prestigious, lucrative posts as President of another college or foundation. Mostly, however, Borchardt was breathing hard down Torrance's own neck; his achievements clouded Torrance's lackadaisical attitude toward his work. The trustees were looking carefully at the Dean. He might not have the elegance of a Torrance, but he had an ability that frightened the older man.

When he turned from the window, Torrance assumed a benign expression: 'You're paranoid, Arnold.'

'Oh? Your ground shifting dangerously under you, Frank?'

A small, cold smile. 'How?'

'You're playing games now.'

'You seem sure of yourself.'

'You know I met with the trustees last week.'

Torrance nodded his head, then he spoke, wearily: 'So?'

'They asked me a great deal about you. How your mood was, working habits, plans, innovative projects . . .'

'The usual check and double check. I know all that.'

'They're shopping for a new President and you know it.'

'Yes and I know you're after it hotter than a stud after a mare in heat. I'm sure I'm not the only one doing a bit of sabotaging around here. So what, Arnold? We know it. We're both playing the game and . . . and . . .' – the President paused dramatically – '. . . you forget I've been playing it a lot longer than you have and much more successfully. If I know anything it's my way around the politics of academe; I'm not worried.'

Borchardt's cold black eyes sparkled. A trace of smile curled inside his beard like a snake stirring in sleep in its nest. Torrance shuddered intuitively. The Dean smiled so seldom, was such a serious young man, that this strange smile bothered him. What was he going to uncoil?

'I didn't play my trump, Frank.'

'You have a trump to play?'

'Linda Kitteredge.'

Yes, he had a trump to play all right. Linda Kitteredge, twenty years old, a Junior pre-med student, involved in Student Theater, beautiful, young, uninhibited, a woman who had tempted the middle-aged university president to break the cardinal rule of campus life: *Thou shalt not sleep with thy students.* The best kept secret since the Manhattan project was no longer such a well-kept secret.

'Bravo, Borchardt. How the hell—'

'—did I find out?' Now the smile blossomed fully. The snake stretched to its full length within its nest. Luxuriant, powerful, sure of its own strength. 'Call it intuition.'

'To hell with intuition. How did you find out?'

'Long story and a piece of luck.'

'The luck first.'

'I was walking by her house at three o'clock the morning of the 17th, two days before the meeting with the trustees. Guess what President of what University was coming out of what co-eds little house?'

'What were you doing there at that hour? Who's house were *you* coming out of?'

'My own. I couldn't sleep. I don't sleep very much. I'm an insomniac. So I walk until I can't hold my head up and then I stagger home to bed.'

Torrance smiled. 'Well . . . well . . .' He paced once around the office, carefully touring behind Borchardt, a tactic he'd learned years back when he was a Freshman Dean at Harvard. Adversaries always feel uneasy when someone is behind them. 'What's the deal, Arnold?'

The snake went back into the bush. 'Clean up this presentation, trade every favor in the book for the Indian Study Center and make me your personal assistant with a promise you'll be out within three years and stop blocking all my applications to other universities.

Torrance lifted an eyebrow. 'Stiff!'

'You've made a big mistake. No one's going to tolerate a college President who screws the students. If this gets out you'll be finished for life. And you know it, Frank!'

'All true. You're a pretty cold young man.'

'I know what I want. I want my own presidency and as your assistant I'll be in position to get one.'

'Oh, yes. No arguments. Do I have time to think?'

'Why not? I admire you for not denying the liasion.'

'If you're going to be a successful administrator, Arnold, learn that success only comes by facing reality hard on! Unblinking. No illusions. Something leaked out of the bucket. Clean it up. Period. Give me a few days. You've rocked my life a bit.'

'No hard feelings?'

'Don't expect brotherly love, Arnold. Now, if you would leave me alone?'

As soon as Borchardt left the room Torrance picked up his private line and dialed Linda Kitteredge's number. He marveled and scolded himself that still, after almost six months of the relationship he, a fifty-seven year old man, prominent, sophisticated and distinguished, should feel butterflies in his stomach and get somewhat shaky, telephoning a young girl. She was – admittedly – very beautiful and (damn it all) exciting. 'Acting like an adolescent with his first love, Crazy . . .' he thought.

The sound of her voice did nothing to settle his nerves. She spoke with a clean high precise tone, at once (if one could imagine it) ambiguous and provocative. Behind every word Linda spoke lay echoes of a dozen winds unspoken, full of mysterious promise.

'You answer the telephone as if you know who's on the other end.'

'Maybe I do.'

'You're frightening. I sometimes think you've lived several whole other lifetimes and they're all coming alive again in your present form.'

'You mean body.'

'I wouldn't deny it. Something's very alive in that body.'

'You think I'm a witch?'

'You're not really twenty, are you? You're two thousand and twenty.'

'You wouldn't want an older woman at your age, would you Frank?'

The sound of his name on her lips made him smile. 'If she looked and acted like you . . . ?'

'I can tell when you've got something to say and don't want to say it.'

'Bright kid. Arnold Borchardt's found out about us.'

'So . . . ?'

'Don't be naive.'

'You just got finished saying I was a kid.'

'I've got to talk to you.'

'You don't want to cool it a while?'

'I can't.'

Her laughter rippled through the phone and into the very marrow of his bones.

'I'll be right over.'

'Hurry. I've got a five fifteen Biology lab.'

President Torrance slowly hung up the telephone. He took a deep breath. Damn Borchardt for mucking up his perfect life!

CHAPTER 2

Torrance was not happy to be hailed coming out of the Administration building. He heard his name flung across the air and pretended to ignore whoever was calling him. Ignorance became impossible the second time. The voice calling him boomed.

Sherman Markham, Dean of the Law school charged toward the President like a mad bear; Markham was a tall muscular man with a wild gray mane of long hippie-styled hair flowing behind him. His voice was a basso profundo that had thundered in many a courtroom. He was considered one of the finest left-wing trial lawyers in America. He used his academic position as a shield to ward off the criticisms of a world that considered radical causes beneath the dignity of a lawyer with Markham's skills. He only defended cases that promised political fall-out. Torrance was afraid that Markham was about to introduce him to one of his new clients. A small, scruffy man in a dirty raincoat trailed after the tall dean. The fellow was obviously ill-at-ease amid the palm trees of Academe. Torrance figured he was some kind of intense, explosive anarchist.

'You've got to meet this man!' Markham enthused. 'He's incredible, Frank. Come here!' he encouraged his guest, who seemed to hang back and drag his heels.

'Another one of your anarchic troublemakers, Sherm?'

'No! He's one of the finest homicide detectives in

America. Lieutenant Columbo, I want you to meet Franklin Torrance, President of Meredith.' Markham beamed with the satisfaction of the man who had just arranged a summit meeting between the leaders of Russia, China and the United States.

Columbo held out his hand, muttered his pleasure and did indeed feel a spot of awe for the distinguished-looking President of Meredith. 'That's some house for California, huh?' he said by way of openers, leaning his head toward the administration building.

Torrance could hardly believe Markham's praise of this man. 'Transported brick-by-brick from Salem, Massachusetts, Lieutenant.'

'Very impressive.' Columbo swayed. This wasn't his world at all.

'Pleasant place to work. Now if you'll excuse me. I'm in a hurry.'

'Busy administrator,' Markham added. 'His job is to keep the money flowing, set academic standards and set examples. Right, Frank. You've got to be the embodiment of academic rectitude?'

'And I presume Lieutenant Columbo here has to be the embodiment of Law Enforcement?' He lifted an eyebrow.

'Well, it is a responsibility, sir, when you represent the department.'

'What brings you to us today? Skeletons in the closet?'

'Lieutenant Columbo is going to address the Law School on Homicide and the Law. I'm just showing him around campus before dinner and the lecture.'

'I don't mind admitting I'm pretty nervous too,' said Columbo. 'I've never talked to more than three people at once in my life.' He shook his head as though to clear it of a bad dream. 'And these law school types are pretty sharp.'

'I'm sure you'll manage Lieutenant. Now if you'll excuse me, I'm on my way to cajole a foundation executive.'

'You go right ahead. Nice meeting you.'

Homicide detective! thought Torrance. He looked like an unemployed numbers runner. Ironic though, that Meredith should have a homicide man on campus today of all days. He smiled. Borchardt had overstepped and something had to be done.

Linda agreed. 'Smarmy little man!'

'Be kind, Linda.'

But she was in no mood to be kind. Torrance sometimes asked himself how he'd allowed himself to become involved with such a cold-blooded girl. She sat on a low bean-bag chair her naked legs tucked up under her, her mini-skirt hiked to the top of her thigh. Her lithe young woman's figure seemed to tremble in front of Torrance's eyes. Looking at her he answered his own question: How could he resist her seductiveness? Surely, she had seduced him. He would never have succumbed to the charms of a student if she hadn't taken the initiative. God knew temptation was all around, but he had resisted for twenty-five years.

This one, Linda Kitteredge, was something else again. She sparkled like a diamond, her eyes flashed with a devastating light. She seemed to hypnotize everyone in her presence. The girl had an overwhelmingly intense inner power. Torrance, in all his years of working and manipulating people had never encountered anyone quite like Linda. She was able to set her mind on something and it happened. And, for some unknown reason, she'd set her mind on Frank Torrance and enthralled him in spite of his position, his twenty-eight-year marriage and everything he'd have to lose.

Looking at Linda now, Torrance hardly regretted his entanglement. Choices were simple in her presence.

'He's a smarmy, ambitious, pawing little man.'

'Pawing?' Torrance's ears picked up.

'Oh, not really. His eyes paw. I can't tell you how many girls tell me they think Borchardt's lurking in the shadows ready to rape them. He gives off that kind of air. Ugh!'

Torrance smiled. 'He's put me on the spot.'

'Just you?'

'Come on now. What do you have to lose if our relationship became common knowledge?'

'Oh, Frank! "Relationship". Quaint academic disguises. You mean if it got out we were sleeping together? Screwing!'

He closed his eyes as though she were taxing his patience. She wasn't of course. He was delighted when she was vulgar. 'I have a great deal to lose. A lifetime's activity, hard work and effort. Respect. I rather like it here.'

'In my house!'

'As President of Meredith.'

'Yeah. Well, I can see that. Lot's of money, contacts, power, prestige. All the establishment crap!'

'Be that as it may, a scandal would destroy me.'

'So destroy him. The little bastard.'

'I've got nothing on him. If I had, I'd use it. I've done it before. I've tried to discredit him in subtle ways, but he's always a jump ahead. Very sharp man, really, Borchardt. And the students – not the females I presume – like him. They think I'm a cold fish.'

'We ought to sell tickets to the show in my bedroom.'

'You're very funny today.'

'I like to stir you up.'

'Enough problems today without that.'

Linda pursed her lips in a pretence of thought. She suggested they kill Borchardt. Just get rid of him. Dump him in the Pacific, push him off the roof of one of the buildings, run him down with Torrance's car . . . she was full of ideas.

'Be serious, Linda. I came here so that you'd help me think my way out of this. Not to get in deeper.'

'I am serious, Frank. We should kill him. Or you should or I should. Actually, I should. Nobody else knows about us, therefore I'd be the perfect person to kill him because no one'd ever suspect me. I'll kill him.'

'How? Gun? Knife? Garotte? Or will you just dazzle him to death with your eyes?'

'Let me think.' She stood up and toured the room. Torrance forgot his problem as he watched her legs stride about, slender, sweetly shaped, unbearably exciting. He had trouble keeping his mind on the business at hand. When he told Linda she informed him she had a Biology Lab. in half an hour and did he want to be responsible for one of his students having a poor attendance record. 'I've got it!' She resumed pacing. Torrance was losing patience.

'For God's sake, Linda. Hurry up.'

'The perfect crime takes a few minutes to think up.' She nibbled her tongue thoughtfully.

When he heard the idea, Torrance had to admit it would probably work. It involved a degree of violence. But Torrance didn't worry about a single violent action. He worried instead that the idea rather thrilled him as it had thrilled Linda. 'What kind of a monstrous pair are we?' he asked himself and chuckled. 'Damned if I don't feel better than I've felt in a long time, you sure you don't want to cut that Lab.?'

'Positive. Come back some other time!'

On his way home he stopped by the faculty club for a swim. He swam with more energy, verve and deep pleasure than he'd experienced in years. It was almost as though he were in training.

CHAPTER 3

The lecture hall was depressingly large and distressingly full. An audience of three hundred and forty law students turned out to hear Columbo speak. Before the lecture began they were noisy, colorful and – to the Lieutenant's ears – as frightening as the crowds in the Roman Coliseum were to the Gladiators.

Columbo stood in a little side room, with Markham making small talk while they waited for the slow, slow minute hand of the clock to settle on the twelve, marking exactly eight p.m. Columbo rocked from his left foot to his right foot and back again, as nervous a race horse as ever entered the starting gate. Whatever Markham was saying did not penetrate the detective's consciousness. All he heard was the frightening din of voices.

'Are you all right, Lieutenant?' Markham's words finally cut through Columbo's haze.

'Oh, yeah! Yeah? That's a good crowd?'

'Exceptional. Homicide is a favored subject.'

'I guess so.'

'No need to be nervous. This is a very sympathetic bunch. Bright too. I love getting up there and really laying it out for them.'

'Yeah. Yeah I can appreciate that Mr Markham, but . . . I've never done this before. I mean . . .' Columbo shook his head from left to right. 'They're all going to have their own opinions.'

'Absolutely! That's the stimulating factor. They let you know it too.'

'That's what I was afraid of.'

On the clock the merciless minute hand hit the twelve. Somewhere on campus a bell tower chimed eight slow majestic peels. Columbo dabbed his forehead and went out onto the lecture platform. Spartacus fed to the lions.

Arnold Borchardt heard the bells peeling eight o'clock and realized that, as usual, he was late to the theater for rehearsals. He quickly stuffed some papers into a briefcase and fled the office. Since his definition of 'late' was to arrive after the director, he could never be late. Though he gave up his teaching duties upon his appointment as Dean of Students, he retained his one commitment to the Drama Department, where, for the past six years, he directed an annual student production drawn from the repertory of 17th-century revenge tragedy.

This year's production, scheduled to open in two nights, was *The White Devil* by John Webster. The play is about a conniving duchess, vengeful men and plotting courtiers all made grand by brilliant poetry and awash with murder and blood. The central character, The White Devil, is Vittoria Corombona, 'a most notorious strumpet' who inspires a train of unnatural deaths.

Borchardt looked to the direction and production of the play as the bright spot in his academic year. As much as his ambition drove him toward administrative work and the political intrigue that went with it, he found that each year's play production put him in touch with all the values and inspirations which first drew him into the academic life. Borchardt was an excellent Elizabethan scholar whose PhD Thesis on *The Politics of Jacobean Melodrama* became a text book and a model for the writing of literary criticism grounded in social history.

Borchardt's true love was the language of the period and the thrilling thunder of the playwrights' lines. He was reminded of this once again as he entered the darkened auditorium and heard Linda Kitteredge playing Vittoria Corombona rehearse with Blake Newman, playing her lover Brachiano. It is their love affair which sets the ball of murder and revenge rolling:

VITTORIA: To pass away the time, I'll tell your grace
A dream I had last night.
BRACHIANO: Most wishedly.
VITTORIA: A foolish idle dream.
Methought I walked about the mid of night
Into a church yard where a goodly yew tree
Spread her large root in ground. Under that yew
As I sat sadly leaning on a grave
Chequered with cross sticks, there came stealing in
Your duchess and my husband: one of them
A Pick axe bore, the other a rusty spade
And in rough terms they 'gan to challenge me
About this yew.
BRACHIANO: That tree?
VITTORIA: This harmless yew:
They told me my intent was to root up

That well grown yew, and plant i' the stead of it
A withered blackthorn; and for that they vowed
To bury me alive. My husband straight
With pick-axe 'gan to dig and your fell duchess
With shovel, like a Fury, voided out
The earth, and scattered bones. Lord, how, methought,
I trembled! And yet, for all this terror,
I could not pray.

BRACHIANO: No, the Devil was in your dream.

VITTORIA: When to my rescue there arose, methought,
A whirlwind, which let fall a massy arm
From that strong plant;
And both were struck dead by that sacred yew,
In that base shallow grave that was their due.

BRACHIANO: Sweetly shall I interpret this your dream.
You are lodged within his arms who shall protect you
From all the fevers of a jealous husband;
From the poor envy of our phlegmatic duchess.
I'll seat you above the law, and above scandal;
Give to your thoughts the invention of delight,
And the fruition—

'Very good you two,' Borchardt shouted from the auditorium. He felt good. His student actors had that natural amateur energy that professionals were often compelled to imitate. They were really into the roles, and he had to admit Linda Kitteredge was so beautiful that it was hard to fault Torrance for his infatuation. The dean wondered idly, however, whether the girl was by nature as cold as Vittoria. She played the part well, with such regal murderous authority, one easily believed her capable of any outrageous action.

Columbo looked out over the sea of young lawyers, thousands of eyes directed toward him. Markham's introduction was effusive, complimentary and difficult for the detective to really believe. He felt himself get hot all over. He knew he should have better control of himself. He was just addressing a bunch of kids. Bright kids though. Awfully bright! Boy, he should have listened to his wife when she asked him why he should give his secrets away to a bunch of students who would only use them against him if they ever had to defend a murderer in court. Columbo had felt some strong sense of duty (and flattery) when asked to speak to the Meredith law school, and so he'd accepted, thoughtlessly, he felt now. Too quickly.

Suddenly he was at the podium, which was too high for him. He tried to peer over it, but knew he couldn't deliver a lecture on tiptoe. So he sidled around to the left of it and began – 'You got to understand I'm not used to—' when he realized that no one heard him. He was standing too far from the microphone.

Markham stood quickly and adjusted it.

Columbo's words: 'Yeah that's better' boomed across the hall and laughter rose from the students. 'I've got some notes here.' Columbo began pawing mechanically, then a little desperately, through his pockets. The laughter increased. 'I'm always writing stuff down and then I can't find it. Oh! Here it is!' He pulled two envelopes and a parking ticket from the inside pocket of his jacket. Notes for his speech were penciled on the back.

'Homicide's murder. That's pretty clear. I mean I don't have to tell you that . . . I don't really know why I made that note. Once there's been a murder the homicide squad's work begins. It's not pretty work right away. First comes all the forensic guys and photographers. You got to keep your eye on everything. I mean everything: I've got kind of a pattern that I use subconsciously, I guess, after all this time, but it works for me. Angles for example. How the body's lying, the position of the limbs, the way the head lies . . . all that . . . very important. Then there's the wound, angles again: how the bullet, knife whatever the weapon was went into the body. You can tell a lot about the killer's relationship to his victim from where he was standing when the shot's fired or whatever. That's a lot of trigonometry and measuring which I'm not too good at, but the forensic guys know what they're doing. They mess around those corpses like dogs around a tree . . . But these angles, tell you how much trust there was between victim and murderer . . .'

One of the female students dropped her head in her hands. Columbo noted it and felt he may have gone too far.

'It's grisly stuff all right, but murder's grisly stuff too . . . and that's really what I want to talk about: the psychology at work between the murderer and the victim—'

*

In the theater the rehearsal was progressing. Borchardt sat in the dark, allowing his cast and crew to play out the whole performance without interruption. He sat with a lighted clipboard on his lap, taking notes. It was the final run through without costume.

Three men are on stage: Brachiano, Flamineo and a Doctor. The lights darken a few shades. Borchardt made a note to slow down the light fade until the last speech before the exit.

FLAMINEO: Look, his eyes' bloodshed, like a needle a surgeon stitcheth a wound with. Let me embrace thee toad, and love thee, O thou abominable loathesome gargarism, that will fetch up lungs, lights, heart and liver, by scruples.

BRACHIANO: No more. I must employ thee honest doctor: you must to Padua and by the way use some of your skill for us.

DOCTOR: Sir, I shall.

BRACHIANO: But, for Camillo?

FLAMINEO: He dies this night by such a politic strain. Men shall suppose him by's own engine slain. But for your duchess' death—

DOCTOR: I'll make her sure.

BRACHIANO: Small mischiefs are by greater made secure.

In the darkened auditorium, Torrance slipped into the seat next to Borchardt.

'How's it going, Arnold?' he whispered.

'These kids aren't bad.'

'Seems like death's in the air.'

'Double murder coming up.'

'I figure I don't have to hide any more rendezvous with Linda from you.'

'She's a good actress. Does she want to make a career of it?'

'She wants to be a doctor–surgeon, I think. Ambitious girl. She'll dump me soon!'

'I'm not backing away, Frank.'

The whispered conversation continued as bloody deeds unfolded on stage.

'Why do you want to ruin me?'

'I want to advance myself. What the hell else do I have in life?'

'Foul tactics, Arnold.'

'Why not? You'll always find a foundation job you're one of the establishment insiders. Shhhh! I've got to take notes. Dress rehearsal's tomorrow.'

Torrance settled more firmly into his seat. 'It's bloody unfair I tell you. You can compromise.'

In the lecture hall Columbo's self-conscious nerve-riddled delivery riveted his audience. His authority over his subject was hypnotic:

'Your first clue's always the body and its surroundings. Even though the body's dead it can be a pretty good witness. You'd be surprised how much a corpse can tell you. Take the room he's killed in for instance. Or she. Sometimes women are killed just like women kill. Well . . . if it's his home (or hers) you've got a lot to go on. Type of person, likes and dislikes, interests, relationships. People put a lot of pictures around: parents, children, cousins, friends . . . you can tell a lot by the pictures. Everything. But what you're really looking for is something a little out of place. Like a very neat house where the ashtray's spilled. I had a case like that. Ashtray was spilled but you could tell that the guy living there was really neat.'

Unconsciously, he patted his raincoat. 'Yeah? Well that was a pretty big tip off: somebody stood up real fast while they were stubbing out a cigarette. Look at the butts and get the brand. Then when you're talking to the suspects – everybody's always a suspect but you've got a thing inside tells you when you're really on the right track – anyhow when you're watching the suspects, get them to smoke. A little trick never hurt anything. Only one person smoked the brand of cigarettes in the ash tray. Anyhow . . . I pursued this one case and I found who smoked the cigarettes in the ash tray. It wasn't any of the suspects. It was the victim. I guess he was the guy who stood up fast when he realized he was about to be killed.'

The audience laughed. Columbo suddenly realized he'd lost his place among the mess of notes. The audience laughed louder. He turned the envelopes in his hand back and forth, but couldn't make out what his notes meant. He had jotted them down over lunch the day before and they were flecked with chile sauce.

'But the principle's O.K. Watching the suspects . . .' He fumbled some more. 'Oh, yeah . . . details. This is a detail business. I tell the young guys coming in to work with me the first time. I tell them to train their eyes. The way a guy stands . . . what's on his clothes . . . shoes . . . shoes are very important . . .' He glanced down at his notes again. 'Shoes . . .'

Toward the end of the last act:

VITTORIA: I'll tell thee what, I will not in my death shed one base tear; or if look pale – for want of blood – not fear.

Torrance leaned over to Borchardt and whispered, 'You've got me over a goddamned barrel.'

'Not my problem. You put yourself there.'

'Have it your way.'

'Does that mean you'll do what I asked?'

'It means you've given me no choices.'

'Sorry. Think twice next time you get involved with another Linda Kitteredge.'

Vittoria Corombona was killed on stage. The lights shifted to a stunning scarlet.

Torrance whispered: 'The trouble with you, Borchardt, is that you're a moralist. You think you're a crusader for right against a world of wrongs. It's how you got your job and it's what will bring you down one day.'

'That's why I love this kind of play. Evil always gets it in the end.' He turned toward Torrance and smiled his reptile smile. 'I'm not evil, Frank.'

'And . . . ?'

'Look at your lady friend die.' Borchardt was chuckling mirthlessly.

Torrance, confirmed in his resolve rose and slipped out of the darkened theater.

After the curtain fell on the scene, Borchardt called for the house-lights to be brought up. Then, in their glare, he called the cast to the front of the stage. They sat there, transformed from Jacobean courtiers back into students. They listened intently to their director's praise and criticism. His notes were surprisingly few for the next to last rehearsal, so Borchardt felt compelled to lecture them on over-confidence. They had a very good production going but they mustn't let it go to their heads. The material was tough and could turn and snap them into the trap of its melodramatic excesses as much as it could carry them to glorious heights of poetry and performance.

Later, Linda Kitteredge lingered backstage, waiting for the rest of the cast and the technicians to leave. She kept a close eye on Dean Borchardt who sat at the multi-levered light board reviewing the many light cues he had personally designed for the performance. Linda sat on a small velveteen hassock amid a clutter of damasks, stage furniture, tables of props and two gilded coffins up on trestles. (These were for the disposition of corpses in two murder-dream sequences.) The apparent clutter was arranged to fulfil the set changes and cues of the play and was no clutter at all, really, but a well-organized scheme for creating artifice and magic on stage.

Linda sat and waited, watching Borchardt with his young light man, a physics major named Peter Arminski, as they ran through each of the lighting changes and made sure they were tied to the specific cue lines. When they were finished Borchardt dismissed Peter and walked out on to the setting for the first scene, a street in Rome, and stood there in the shadow of a single light bulb looking out toward the empty auditorium. It is a special peace one feels onstage, alone, with only an imaginary audience seated in the empty house listening to your thoughts.

Linda waited as the light man left the theater. He walked within a few yards of where she was seated and seemed to hesitate a moment. Then he left. She waited a moment before speaking Borchardt's name. The Dean was startled. 'I didn't know any one was still here, Linda.' He walked off-stage and into the wing with her. He was angry at having had his reverie interrupted.

'It's hard for me to leave, Dean Borchardt. I was sitting back there dreaming.'

'Me too, Linda. I once played a season of summer stock and the last thing I ever wanted to do was leave the theater after performances every night. But I left for good. I became a professor and then even left that behind.'

'Do you think I'd ever have a future as a professional actress?'

Borchardt smiled knowingly. How many students had expressed the same star-struck notion? 'It's wonderful fun. But it's a very tough racket.'

Linda stood and moved toward the stage again, so that Borchardt was forced to turn his back to the stage door.

'Can you tell anything at all from a college actress?' she conferred. 'I mean about talent and futures and a career?'

'It's a bit early, Linda. There's no telling what training and practice and exposure will do for you.'

Just then Torrance stepped out of the shadows and brought a heavy piece of lead pipe crashing into Borchardt's skull behind his left ear. The dean emitted a low, grunt-like groan and collapsed amid the seventeenth-century furnishings.

'Very nice! Neat as a pin, Mr President.' Linda came forward and looked down at the limp man.

'He's still alive.' Torrance disappeared backstage a moment, then returned.

'Where did you go?'

'I put the pipe back into a box full of pipes, clamps and stuff. Very handy tools they keep back here.'

'Did you wipe off any finger prints?'

'Linda, love, I'm considered a very intelligent and educated man by my peers.'

'Can't hurt to ask. Now what?'

'Are those coffins real?'

'Uh-huh. Louise . . . the prop girl . . . got them on loan from a mortuary supply store.'

'I suggest we put the poor old dean in one of those, fasten the clamps and let nature do the rest of our work. Nothing more airtight!'

'Maybe you're as intelligent as you say.'

Torrance opened one of the two coffins and then picked Borchardt up under the arms. Linda took his feet. As they dropped the unconscious academic into the plush-lined box, Torrance said: 'I'm not going to miss the man a bit.' He slammed down the coffin cover and clamped it into place. Then he took his handkerchief from his pocket and wiped the box clean. Turning to Linda as he pocketed the handkerchief he said: 'That takes care of that. He never knew what hit him. May I take you home?'

'I'd be delighted,' she answered.

And they left the theater.

Columbo was sitting on the edge of the stage in the Law School Lecture hall. He had been answering questions happily for the last quarter hour. The students had warmed to his personality, and were entering into enthusiastic dialogue with him. They were clamoring all over one another shouting 'Lieutenant!' 'Columbo!' 'Sir!' Markham beamed on the dias. Columbo raised his hands over his head. 'Hey! Quiet. O.K. Take it easy. One at a time!'

When the crowd had settled down Columbo

addressed them: 'You've been really great. I want you to know that. I don't give many talks to a lot of people. I don't really get out in public much. But if you guys – and ladies there – are the future lawyers of America . . . well . . . that's wonderful. There's something I've got to say about people who kill before we're finished here. Something you lawyers should know. That is that a lot of people that commit murder aren't bad people. I know that sounds funny; but a lot of times it's people who have just gone about as far as they can go and get desperate. I don't condemn murderers just like that, understand. They're victims just like the people they kill and they're going to need the best you lawyers can give them when their time comes. I hope that's clear.'

When he stood to join Markham on the dias, the auditorium erupted in applause and cheers.

'That's pretty great,' Columbo mumbled to Markham as they left the hall. 'That's a terrific bunch you've got there.'

CHAPTER 4

Faculty and students milled about holding paper cups of punch in their hands. The noise of conflicting conversations was deafening. Sherman Markham carried a small plate of tiny sandwiches: devilled egg, caviare, tuna-salad. Members of the Law Faculty punched him on the shoulder, slapped him on the back, but Markham managed to contain the sandwiches and punch so nothing spilled. Congratulations over Columbo's formidable success was enthusiastic and voluble.

The object of this adulation sat quietly in a corner, watching the carousing of the students and faculty. 'Boy, these people really let themselves go,' he thought to himself. Columbo had never known that the groves of academe were so full of cavorting beasts as these. No dry dusty bookworms in this room! They were drinking, joking and showing affection as heartily as any group he'd ever seen. Markham thrust a cup of punch and plate of sandwiches at him.

'Hey, look at that!' Columbo studied the assortment of little culinary dots that studded his plate. 'You wouldn't have a bowl of chili around would you?'

'Lieutenant! You're an original. No. I'm afraid we don't. Just these finger sandwiches. Delicate, eh?' He laughed.

'Finger sandwiches?'

'That's what these are called. Finger sandwiches. Canapés . . .'

'You've got to excuse me, Mr Markham, but I don't

have the best education. I went to college all right and didn't do too badly. But my wife, she's the reader in the family. I don't have time to read much. It's a pain to me . . . I'd like very much to improve myself.'

'You don't need improvement, Lieutenant. As a lawyer, now, I want to tell you, I'd hate to come up in court against any case you'd been responsible for preparing. You don't seem to miss a trick. What you said in your lecture was illuminating. I hope the students learn a bit from it.'

'That's the practical side, but when it comes to theory . . .'

A hush fell on the room. Not a total blackout of sound, but a movable stillness rippling from one group to another. The President of the University, Torrance was standing in the doorway. Protocol required Markham to greet him. He excused himself from Columbo.

The detective watched fascinated as the Law School Dean greeted the University President and led him to the refreshment table. A bit like a court, where people pay their respects to the first among them. Everyone watched the little charade and then the buzz of conversation picked up again.

The young woman student who'd almost fainted during Columbo's speech approached him. 'Excuse me, Lieutenant. I wanted to tell you how much I enjoyed the lecture.'

'Aren't you the lady that almost—?'

'Yes.' She smiled sheepishly. 'I'm ashamed to admit the truth. But I suddenly had this horrible picture in my mind . . .'

'Excuse me, Lieutenant,' Markham interrupted, 'but President Torrance says he's dying to talk to you.'

'Excuse me,' Columbo left the girl and began pushing through the crowd, following Markham.

Torrance stood near the refreshments aglow with vitality. Every hair in perfect place.

Columbo, however, noticed a greasy shine near the bottom of Torrance's left cheek. He couldn't quite make it out: a kind of tanned powder, slight grease or cold cream content, drying into caked flakes. It wasn't a scab. It was some kind of make up. Funny, he thought, maybe the guy's really vain and covering up some kind of mole, blemish or birth mark.

Torrance was a bundle of energies and enthusiasm. His words tumbled over one another like beans spilling from a sack: 'I've been wanting to talk ever since we met, Lieutenant. I hear terrific things. Great things. Fabulous. You're supposedly the best. The very best in your field. I like that. If we taught criminology and homicide detection here I'd offer you a job; maybe I should offer you one in any case. How would you like to hold a seminar in homicide? I can see the catalogue now: Homicide 403, Lieutenant Columbo, three credits. A murder will be committed by a student in the course of each week and the other members in the seminar will be required to detect it. Of course the victims must not be other seminar members or you'd lose a significant enrolment by the end of the quarter.' He laughed at his own wit. 'I like that don't you Sherman.' Torrance clapped the Law School Dean on the back. 'But really, Columbo, tell me. How do you track the culprits down?'

'It's all got to do with the special case, Mr Torrance. Each thing's different.'

'He's been brilliant,' Markham threw in. 'Incredible! Details. Details. He watches them like a hawk tracks a field mouse. Circle and watch and then dive! Isn't that it, Lieutenant?'

'It's pretty hard to generalize, Mr Markham.'

'And he's modest too, Frank. We've had a great evening. I'm sorry you missed it.'

'I can't be everywhere all the time, Sherman. But I am sorry I missed it, Columbo. I think we could all benefit from the kind of perception you bring to your subject. It's hot in here.' Torrance turned back to the punch bowl and, as if to confirm what had just been said, Columbo noticed a sticky white powder on the tips of his black shoe. Torrance had been walking somewhere where there was resin.

Torrance turned back to Columbo. 'Tell me about motiveless crime, Lieutenant? Have you ever tracked a murderer who just at random shot somebody for no reason at all? They don't know each other; the victim or the murderer? They've no acquaintanceship, nothing. The weapon is something undistinguished. No bullets to trace, or real wounds. Let's say a baling hook . . . no that's already identifiable . . . a heavy stick. How would you go about cracking that one?'

'That's hard Mr Torrance. Mostly you've got to have a motive. Or a relationship.'

'*Crimes passionel!*'

'I don't quite follow you.'

'Man finds wife in bed with best friend. Shoots wife or best friend or both. That's a crime of passion. Justifiable homicide in French law. We're not that civilized yet in America.' He stuffed another sandwich into his mouth. 'I am hungry!'

'Doesn't sound too hard to solve,' Columbo tried to joke.

'Nope. It's all out front there. Good crowd you have,

Sherman. How do you trace a weapon Columbo? Say a blunt instrument?'

'Usually fingerprints, possession or not at all. That's a very hard piece of work, Mr Torrance. With a bullet there's ballistics, but anything else . . . ?' He shrugged.

'Fascinating! Quite a way to make a living. I should have written detective fiction. I'd have enjoyed that instead of all this hob-nobbing around running universities, attending parties, raising money, dining out . . . it's very hard on the nerves. You're really just a hunter aren't you Columbo? A basset or hound tracking the quarry to its lair!'

'My wife says I remind her of a basset. Funny thing. That's just the kind of dog we have.'

'Tracking the quarry to its lair!' Torrance took a deep gulp of the red punch. 'Yes, Lieutenant. And yet I'd say there must be times when the police with all their scientific devises. All their skill and experience fail—?'

'Yes, sir. That's very true. There are things we can't always lick—'

'Scholars think themselves into blind alleys too, Lieutenant.'

'I'm sure that's correct, sir.'

'Of course there couldn't be a perfect crime any more than there's a perfect soap bubble or a perfect heart . . .'

'It's my experience, sir, that there's always something a little wrong that's the tip-off. Even a thread or a hair . . . one hair . . .' Columbo looked around the room and noticed the crowd thinning. 'You can read a lot of things in a single hair, Mr Torrance.'

'There's no question, then, Lieutenant, that to commit a perfect crime, the murderer must be bald, bald as a billiard ball, bald as a bald eagle, bald as the brass balls over a pawn shop . . . pawn shop bald . . . yes! Well, I must be off. More miles to go before I sleep. Goodnight.'

Torrance faded into the crowd, appeared again like a swimmer breaching a wave and disappeared outside the door.

Soon after, when Columbo was walking across the parking lot to his car, he thought about how many people were interested in murder. It wasn't surprising. A murderer crossed over from civilized life into the wilderness. There was nothing more fascinating. He was glad there was some law and order, otherwise he'd have just too much work to do tracking down all those secret murderers when they came out of the closet and did their thing.

CHAPTER 5

Every morning at six-thirty Frank Torrance leapt into his swimming pool. The morning after the murder was no exception. He was into the pool and swam a good strong thirty lengths before breakfast. It seemed to him that every anxiety and tension rolled off his back with each stroke so that he began the day with an inner calm and peacefulness that (he flattered himself) gave him strength for the problems that would inevitably arise within the coming twenty-four hours.

Hilda Torrance, a handsome fifty-two-year-old woman, sat in a deck chair watching her husband's vigorous exertions. She sipped a tall glass of orange juice which in former times would have contained a liberal lacing of vodka. Hilda shifted in and out of periods of acute alcoholism. She was presently out of one. She studied her husband's muscular body and his vigorous swimming, realizing that she had not kept up with him physically during the thirty years of their marriage. On the other hand, she felt that she had matured emotionally more than he. She was a thoughtful intelligent woman who accepted the inevitable ageing that comes with each birthday as a necessarily unavoidable part of life. She didn't like it, but she could live with it. Frank resisted getting older and that resistance could only bring him harm. 'Better to accept what you are: gray hair, wrinkles, sagging breasts and varicose veins, than fight for eternal youth and lose . . .'

she said at one time. 'Everyone comes a cropper sooner or later.'

Torrance pulled himself out of the water and planted himself firmly in front of Hilda as he patted himself dry with the large bath towel. 'Nothing beats that! I've been thinking Hildy, babe, I've got to go to London and Rome during the intersession for a couple of boring conferences. After they're over why don't you meet me in Capri or Ibiza or something and we take ourselves a long overdue fifth honeymoon and vacation?'

'What is this? Be charitable to your wife week?'

'Knock it off, Hildy. I was just thinking we haven't had any real fun in a long time. So, before it's too late . . .'

'Intimations of mortality old fellow.' She sipped. 'Is superman feeling the breath of the grave on those prickly little hairs on the back of his neck?'

'I don't know it's my fate to be attracted to adder-tongued women.'

Hildy smiled maternally, 'It's a nice offer . . . a lovely and a beautiful offer. I accept. But: I can't understand why, all of a sudden . . . this little burst of sunshine after such a long and cloudy period.'

He sat down on the other side of the table. 'Any juice left for the old guy?'

When Hildy returned from the kitchen with a large glass of juice for Torrance and an unbuttered slice of whole wheat toast, Torrance continued: 'You're right about the breath on the back of the neck. We're getting older . . . yes, *I* am saying it. We are getting older. Sixty is creeping over the horizon faster than I'd care to acknowledge. Old and not necessarily wiser. Life is too precious to waste. So . . . ? I want to have some fun, honey. Forget my troubles for a while; chase the pressures away, forget all those ambitions that drove me this far and just relax. Enjoy the old world for a month or so.'

'What happened?' Hildy asked the question with a deadly sober voice. 'Something must have happened or you wouldn't shift gears so fast. Death was always something for the other guy. Suddenly you tell me you've been thinking. I know you too well, Frank.'

'A college friend. You didn't know him. He wasn't even a close acquaintance. I heard yesterday . . . my age . . . dropped dead in the street.' He snapped his fingers. 'Like that. It's always the most absurd things that set you to thinking. It set me thinking.'

'Well, well.' Hildy stared out across the pool, traced the line of an hibiscus with her eye. 'Would you take me to Russia?'

'Why not?'

'I've always wanted to see old waxen-faced Lenin in his tomb. And the place where Peter the Great hung the heads of the nobles along the Kremlin wall. How would that be for fun? After your stints in London and Rome?'

'You've got a date, sweetheart. Meet you under the Kremlin tower, eight o'clock, August 18.'

She laughed, but something nagged at her. There was something deeply wrong and she wondered what it was. She *did* know her husband well, and if he was admitting this much fear, the real fear was very deep and in a man of his strength and optimism it was inspired by some very deep shock. She wondered how long it would be before he either told her what it was or she figured it out for herself.

'Not a happy day, Mr Torrance!' Miss Purdom greeted him soberly as he entered his office.

'Thanks for the wake-up smile!' His heart skipped a beat. They've found Borchardt he thought. Out loud he said: 'What's the terrible news?'

'Look.' Miss Purdom handed him the student newspaper, *The Meredith News* (some called it the *Meredith Mudslinger*). A front page headline read:

TIME FOR TORRANCE TO RESIGN:
FRONT PAGE EDITORIAL.

He could hardly restrain his delight that it wasn't the discovery of Borchardt's body.

'You looking for an early retirement?' Miss Purdom said. 'Why the big grin?'

'It's reached the proportions of a joke.'

'Oh, don't underestimate the kids, Mr Torrance. Dean Borchardt ought to be licking his chops over this one this morning.'

'It's periodic, Purdy. Relax. I'm going to have a meeting with the trustees next week. There's a lot of right in this thing. I have been hard to reach. They were right to bring Arnold in as dean. He's got a wonderful touch with the kids. Now it's for me to change my ways some and take initiatives with the students. Even an old dog can change . . .'

But before attacking his correspondence, he carefully read and re-read the article. It was extremely well-written for a piece of student journalism. In spite of the subject matter, the style made him feel proud. His students really were learning something! His mind strayed to Linda. Strange girl! He wondered what she might be learning. She was an excellent biology student; she had a gift for science and she was a more than passable student actress. He was pleased that he sometimes thought about her from a father's rather than a lover's point of view.

The morning passed with dictation to Miss Purdom, several calls, and the usual check on university departments. After a quick glance at the last of the overnight reports, Torrance wondered what was going on at the theatre. Probably nothing yet. No one would be preparing for the night's dress rehearsal until morning classes were complete.

Miss Purdom rang the intercom. 'Mr Torrance! Do you have any idea where Dean Borchardt is? He's already missed two appointments and he hasn't called in. We tried his house but he's out and his wife seems to have stepped out. I wondered if he'd said anything to you.'

'Not at all, Miss Purdom. Doesn't Miss Schlesinger know?'

'She asked me to ask you.'

'Let me know if he hasn't come within the hour.'

He clicked off the intercom. He wished they'd discover the body so that at least that much of the thing could be over with.

At 11.30 Miss Purdom presented herself with Dean Borchardt's secretary, Miss Schlesinger. She was a tiny sparrow of a woman, under five feet tall, thin as twigs. She wore thick spectacles and was very shy. Torrance looked up from a complex Defense Department report about Research and Development grants to Meredith College. 'No Borchardt?'

'No, sir!' Miss Schlesinger's voice was beautiful. Whoever talked to her on the other end of the telephone must have imagined a robust sensual beauty on her end.

'Have you reached Mrs Borchardt?'

'Yes, sir. She's very worried. The Dean did not show up at home last night.'

'When did you find this out?'

'About half an hour ago.'

'Why didn't somebody tell me?'

'I didn't want to disturb you?'

'My Dean of Students doesn't show up at home during an entire night and you don't want to disturb me? That, Miss Schlesinger, if you didn't know it, is an emergency. Let me talk to Mrs Borchardt myself.'

Annette Borchardt was very concerned. Torrance asked, his voice, low and serious, whether Arnold had been out all night before. (It was common knowledge that the marriage was breaking up, yet Borchardt and Annette remained the closest friends. The split had not yet occurred and Arnold had always come home in the evenings.)

Torrance instructed Miss Purdom to call the police.

'Is that necessary?'

'He's missing. There's no word. Of course it's necessary. Now leave me alone. I've got a meeting with five pentagon idiots at lunch and I've got to prepare my sales pitch.'

But Torrance's concentration was off. He kept thinking about the body, lying like a time bomb at the theater. When it was discovered emotional explosions would rock the university.

He called Linda. She was her usual mildly amused self, though breathless from running from a class. 'Who's going to open a prop coffin so fast? Relax. Enjoy all the important things you have to do. We're home, free.' Her laugh rang across the line. 'I don't even feel connected to it. Know what I mean? It wasn't me doing it – it was somebody else. It's just like acting a part, Frank.

Act the University President. God knows University Presidents don't knock off their deans too often.' Her laughter was exciting. The girl was a kind of Siren, and he had no control over his feelings for her. It delighted and frightened him.

Torrance decided to walk to his faculty club luncheon with the generals by way of the theatre. Inside he found a few student technicians spot painting flats, replacing a few light jells that had faded during the week of rehearsals. A few girls were sewing last minute corrections into the costumes. The prop girl was carefully counting swords, daggers, and jeweled boxes of various sizes. The President said a few kind words to each and circled around the coffin. He could hardly believe Borchardt was inside. But the big box was still clamped as tight as when he and Linda left it the night before.

'Are these the real things?' he asked the prop girl. She assured him it was. 'You want me to show you the inside, Mr Torrance?' He begged off pretending superstitious fear, backing away from the coffin.

As he walked on to the faculty club he felt a bit easier. If it took this long to find the body, no one would ever find out who committed the murder.

CHAPTER 6

When Torrance returned from lunch, Miss Purdom stopped him in the hallway on his way into his own office. 'The lions are waiting for you.'

Again he felt anxious. 'Lions? What lions?' Visions of police flooded into his head.

'A group of students following up on the editorial. They're dead serious about your resigning, boss.'

'Nonsense.' Again he laughed.

'I don't see how you can take it so calmly.'

'Crisis is my middle name, Purdy. See if they want coffee or cokes or something. I'll check with Miss Schlesinger.'

'There's nothing more on Dean Borchardt.'

Miss Schlesinger confirmed Miss Purdom's comment. She had talked twice more with Mrs Borchardt. The police had sent two patrolmen, but no one could tell them much of anything so they'd returned to their beat and were awaiting further developments.

'Maybe he went fishing.'

'He never went fishing!' Miss Schlesinger barked sternly.

'He never disappeared like this.'

'I'm sure there's good reason, Mr Torrance.'

'I'm worried, Miss Schlesinger. Frankly. I'll feel much better when he shows up or we hear from him.'

'I don't see what there is to worry about. The campus community is very safe.'

'These are wild times, Miss Schlesinger. Anything can happen.'

A student delegation of three men and three women waited for him in his office. They all looked very serious; they were neatly dressed, not a pair of blue jeans among them. 'Very serious business,' thought Torrance noting the absence of denim. They had declined refreshment from the enemy and so sat with hands either folded or awkwardly plucking the arms of chairs.

Torrance slipped behind his desk. 'Can't I offer you people anything?'

'Just your resignation, Mr Torrance.' The speaker was an earnest young man with blond hair almost down to his shoulders.

'These things are always conducted a bit more diplomatically,' Torrance said. 'Why don't you tell me your names?'

The blond spokesman was Norman Pejori. A red-haired girl with freckles, Frankie Latourette was co-spokesperson.

Torrance seized the initiative. His experience would overwhelm these children in a moment. 'I read the editorial this morning with great care. In fact I read it twice. I believe there are four points against me.'

Pejori spoke firmly and slowly: 'Your conduct during the student uprisings in 1968.'

'I believe none of you were students here at that time.'

'That's correct, sir. But we've made a thorough study of your stiff attitude toward the students. I believe you called in the local police.'

'I called in fourteen extra police from the city to assist the campus police who were understaffed.'

'And they used tear gas?'

'When the students broke down the doors downstairs and occupied Meredith Hall, tear gas was used.'

'There you are,' M/s Latourette declared.

'Not completely. You've done your research but not all of it. None of you has ever heard my side of the story. There was a caretaker in the building at the time. Someone hit him over the head with a crowbar. He was seriously injured and the rebel students wouldn't allow help to reach him . . . I assume they thought he was me.' Torrance smiled at the idea that a custodian could be mistaken for President of the University. His audience cracked not one smile among them. The President settled in his chair for a long tough afternoon.

In the Meredith theatre, a Mexican-American sophomore named Carlos Asuelo finished sweeping the stage clean. He walked through the prop area off the right side of the stage, past the tables of swords, fans, goblets, plates, daggers and other implements, past the coffins to a broom closet. He stowed his broom and removed a large box of resin which he used to sprinkle the stage so that the actors wouldn't slip and fall during the performance.

He stopped by the caskets and decided that he would resin the stage later. He returned to the broom closet, opened it up and removed a small hand vacuum cleaner which he plugged into an outlet next to the closet. He opened the first of the two coffins and vacuumed the red plush clean.

After carefully closing the first coffin, he tried to open the second and was surprised to find it had been latched. He unlocked the latches and opened the huge box.

Borchardt's dead face was blue from suffocation. His features were lacerated and streaked with dried blood where he had scratched and torn at himself in his death agonies. His right hand was crooked and frozen with rigor mortis. His left clutched the folds of his pants. The dead eyes stared into the flies and beyond.

The meeting in the President's office was now going better than either students or Torrance had expected. The President and the six representatives were engaged in a heated but friendly discussion on administrative responsibilities. Frankie Latourette was vehement in blaming Torrance for not having this same kind of conversation four years ago.

'Four years ago,' he answered, 'we were all younger and less wise. How old were you four years ago?'

'Fifteen.'

'Could you have had such an intelligent input then?'

'No, sir. But you were already a University President.'

'Schooled in old and it seems worn out traditions. Mature people have as much to learn as the young. Perhaps more sometimes since we have as much to unlearn as we learn.'

'The basic problem exists,' a compact little black-haired girl spoke.

'Remoteness?'

'Yes, sir.'

'Why don't we see what the next few months bring. I'm aware of the problem. I don't want to dodge it. Meeting you is part of my facing up. A few months ago I'd have tiptoed away from an encounter of this kind.'

An ashen-faced Miss Purdom opened the door. 'Excuse me, Mr Torrance, but . . .' Tears started from her eyes as she walked across the room. She handed Torrance a piece of paper.

'This is it,' he thought. He hoped his face showed mild curiosity. 'What's the matter, Miss Purdom?'

'Dean Borchardt . . .' She could say no more. She handed Torrance the note paper. He glanced at it and then with a choked voice told the student delegation that their popular dean had been found murdered in the Student Theatre.

CHAPTER 7

Carlos Asuelo sat on the steps outside the theatre in front of the box office. After opening the coffin he had been sick and was now sitting out in the sunshine trying to recover himself. He was pale. The sun felt cold. He had trouble bringing the scene developing around him into focus.

Police emergency vehicles, two patrol cars and an ambulance stood in the driveway and theater parking lot. A police team had already cordoned off the entire area. A small crowd of students and passers-by stood behind the ropes.

Technicians from homicide seemed to be everywhere, inside and out. Carlos had been told not to leave without informing a policeman. He hardly had the strength to move.

Carlos watched as a battered old Mercedes-Benz chugged to a stop behind the police vehicles. There was a pause after the engine was turned off before a short man in a rumpled raincoat chewing on the remnants of a cigar came into view on the far side of the car. Instead of rushing into the theatre, Columbo just stood looking around. He took in the onlookers, stared a moment at Carlos, glanced at the theatre and up and down the street. Then he walked slowly toward Carlos, but his eyes shifted from the boy to the bushes, the grass, the driveway as though he were looking for something he might have lost.

'Hi, kid. You the one found the body?'

Carlos nodded.

'Kind of shakes you up. I know.'

'I don't feel so good. You with the police?'

'Lieutenant Columbo. Homicide.'

'You the detective on the case?'

'Looks like it. Tell me what happened?'

'Not much, Lieutenant. I was cleaning everything up. I'm on the stage crew. I opened one of the coffins up to vacuum it and . . .' Carlos swallowed hard. Columbo patted him on the shoulder. 'That's O.K. I'll go see for myself.'

Backstage the theater was swarming with patrolmen, technicians, detectives. The body had not been moved. It lay like a grotesque full-sized puppet, the attitude still as Carlos had found it. The only concession to sensibility being that someone had closed the eyes so that the dead man's stare would not hypnotize any onlookers.

A police photographer snapped pictures of the corpse and the area. A laboratory man was dusting everywhere for finger-prints although no one doubted so many prints would be found that none could be separated out as belonging to the killer.

Columbo worked his way through the activity to the coffin. He stood a long time staring at the lacerated blue features of the victim. Fingernails buried in the flesh of the cheeks. Coagulated streaks of blood. The gentian blue color of suffocation and rigor mortis. The left hand clutching the left pant leg like a falcon's claw around a rodent's skin. The feet splayed outward. On the shoes a white powdery substance which, when Columbo touched it, proved to be slightly sticky. Resin.

Columbo jotted the last fact down in his notebook

and tried to recall when and where he had recently seen the same thing.

He approached one of the patrolmen standing guard at the stage door. 'Lieutenant Columbo, Homicide.'

'Lieutenant, sir! Everything in order, sir?'

'Oh, yeah. Looks O.K. You the guy who was called in when the kid found the body?'

'We'd already been called by the administration. Dean Borchardt had been missing all day.'

'He's been dead a while alright. Must have been sometime last night.' Funny thought Columbo. He, himself, had been on campus then.

'We were looking for him. That is keeping a lookout for him. Somebody thought he might have gone fishing.'

'Who was that?'

'One of the administration, I guess. I'm not really sure.'

'Thanks.'

Columbo taking in all the props, swords especially, moved over to the head forensics man, Hearn. 'What do you think?'

'Blow behind the left ear, Lieutenant. Cause of death: suffocation. He was stunned, locked in there and had a pretty bad time of it for a couple of minutes.'

'When do you think it happened?'

'By the condition of the body I'd say sometime last night. I'll have a pretty exact time after the autopsy.'

'Yeah. How come he didn't knock the coffin off the trestles when he was wrestling around?'

'No room to maneuver.'

Columbo nodded to himself and moved around the backstage area. It was small and cramped with all the police apparatus there along with the props and stage settings. He drifted back for another look at the body, but found it unpleasant. He'd seen what he needed to see.

'O.K. if we take him away, Lieutenant?'

Columbo nodded. This wouldn't be easy. The back door of the theater was constantly open. Students could come and go; why not any intruder? A stranger off the street?

Torrance walked in just as the coffin was being carried out. Seeing Columbo he crossed the length of the back stage area in two strides. He was very pale. 'Lieutenant! I'm sure you didn't think you'd be back officially like this.'

'Yeah. This is pretty rotten.'

'What happened?'

Columbo studied the President's face. He seemed genuinely unhappy. His eyes were a little wild. He was sweating. 'This Mr Borchardt . . . what is he again?'

'Dean of Students.'

'Yeah. Dean of Students. Somebody hit him behind the ear and knocked him out. Put him into one of those coffins . . . those are for the play I guess.'

'Yes. It's a Jacobean melodrama.'

'A Jacobean . . . I don't get that.'

'A play written in the reign of King James the second of England. Bloody melodramas were all the rage in those days.'

'Is that right? I'm always learning something. That'd explain the coffin then?'

'A prop for the play.'

'Yeah. And Mr Borchardt? He had something to do with all this?' Columbo indicated the theatre.

'He directed one play a year.'

'And this one's it. What's it called?'

'*The White Devil* by John Webster.'

Columbo made a note. 'Well. I was saying. Whoever it was put him in one of those coffins and he suffocated to death.'

'Do you think they meant to kill him?'

'It's a bad joke putting a guy into a sealed coffin.'

'I just don't like to believe that a murder could take place at Meredith.'

'I know what you mean. You got any idea who might've wanted to do this kind of thing?'

'Borchardt was an unpleasant man, Lieutenant, but an excellent dean. He may have had enemies.'

'You got any idea?'

'I wish I did. This is very upsetting.'

'Oh, yeah. It's an awful thing. A man like that. With learning . . .'

'Anything I or my office can do, feel free to ask.'

'I appreciate that.' Columbo scratched his head. 'I don't know where I'm going to start on this . . .'

'Just follow your own lecture notes.'

'What's that?'

'Your lecture. Last night? At the Law School?'

'Oh, yeah! That's right, my own rules. That's not a bad idea!'

'Then if you'll excuse me, there are going to be a lot of questions to answer . . .'

'Funny thing about Borchardt. He has some funny powder on his shoes, sticky . . .'

'Look at your own shoes Lieutenant.'

Columbo looked down. Indeed the tips of his scuffed unpolished shoes had the same powder.

'Resin. The stage is sprinkled with it so that the actors won't lose their footing and hurt themselves.'

'I never knew that.'

'Common procedure, Lieutenant.'

'Right. I'll make a note of that.'

Torrance excused himself. He disappeared in the direction of the stage and auditorium; to comfort the students and theater staff who were shaken.

Columbo glanced straight up at the flies. Pulleys, lines, weights, wires, spot lights, pieces of flat scenery hung above his head, high in the loft. He looked down at the trestles, walked around them, thinking. He looked at the floor . . . footprints, yes, from the resin, but all muddled by so many people coming and going.

He moved toward the back of the prop area into a twilight zone of flats, workbenches, paints and ropes. Boxes of equipment stood against the brick outer wall of the building. A detective stood in the shadows, writing in a note book. Columbo asked him what he thought?

'Clubbed and stuffed into the coffin. Clear as that.'

Columbo nodded agreement. 'Murder weapon?'

'Blunt instrument. Anything. Wrench. Hammer. Lead pipe. There are a lot of things in those wooden boxes over there, Lieutenant Columbo.'

The wooden boxes were filled with foam rubber, cushions, bits of cloth, cotton batting, and – in two of them – tools and lead pipe. Columbo stared down at the lead pipe: 'What's that used for?'

'It fits together like plumbers' stuff. They use it for supports, props, repairs. It's all the same size, see Lieutenant?'

Columbo nodded. 'Better have the lab. look it all over.' He walked back to the murder site, studying the floor, the trestles, the flies again and finally walking the path to the stage back and forth several times.

*

The crowd outside the theatre had been growing. As classes were dismissed the students congregated around the police lines to stare at the scene of the crime. A murmur went up when the coffin was carried out and put into a police station wagon. Another rustle whirred through the crowd when President Torrance came out of the building. He walked straight to the street and climbed into his car without saying a word to anyone.

Linda Kitteredge, who had just come from a Humanities section, watched him. She liked his intrinsic authority; the sense that he was in full command. When the detective in the rumpled and dirty raincoat came out of the theatre, and stopped and stared at the crowd, Linda felt, for an instant that he was looking directly at her. She scoffed at her own imagination. But when Columbo crossed the lawn toward her (and the crown) she felt herself go cold. 'Control yourself. This is all a game,' she whispered to herself.

Columbo unhooked the rope barrier and announced that anyone having legitimate business in the theater could go in now. Linda passed him without a word or a look. He decided to take another look at the corpse. The corpse lay on a stretcher inside the police wagon, next to the coffin.

Columbo pulled back the sheet covering Borchardt's face. He looked carefully at the wound. The skull was partially crushed, just behind the ear, very little of the skin was cut, though there was a deal of swelling. After he'd been hit, he was lifted into the coffin which was on the trestles. Two people. Two people, lifted . . . Columbo made note that somewhere on the body, in the clothing there might lie the one clue he was looking for.

He covered the face and left the wagon. He wasn't

thinking about the lead pipe or wrench or whatever it was that the killer used to club the man. He was thinking that to sneak up that close behind someone, meant that the victim was distracted, concentrating elsewhere. Probably one of the two killers was talking to Borchardt when the other brought the instrument down on the dean's head. Whoever Borchardt was talking to was a friend, acquaintance, because he was totally relaxed. From the position of the wound it was clear that the dean never even looked around at his killer.

By four o'clock the entire cast and crew had gathered for the dress rehearsal that was planned for that night. They sat onstage in casual clothes murmuring and whispering among themselves. Several of the girls were crying and daubing their eyes. The assistant director, Duane Andrus, stood with the stage manager, a girl named Mary Jane Francis. They were trying to decide whether to go ahead with the dress rehearsal.

Finally Andrus, tall, lean, bulging adams' apple, turned to the cast and put the question to them. Did they want to go ahead with the dress rehearsal and the performances of the play or should they cancel the whole thing in honor of Dean Borchardt? The boy who would play Camillo, said that it would be a finer memorial to go on for Borchardt.

One of the girls blurted out 'How could you?'

'If this were professional theatre we'd just go on. I've read about people dropping dead in the middle of performances and the performance went on.'

The boy who would play Flamineo, Vittoria's brother, muttered 'Damned difficult. Makes you feel like a vulture!'

Another girl broke into loud sobs.

'Let's keep this orderly,' said Andrus. 'I think we should go ahead but before the curtain goes up one of us should go out and announce to the audience that we're performing in memory of Dean Borchardt. Linda? You're the lead. Would you do it?'

Columbo, who had been prowling around the theatre finding out what he could, stood in the wings listening to the cast's deliberations. He hadn't noticed Linda before. She had been standing alone very near the opposite wing, almost out of sight. Now when she stepped forward, Columbo couldn't help noticing how beautiful she was, how gracefully she moved across the stage, and how self-possessed she was.

'I don't mind.' She addressed Andrus. 'Will you or somebody write out what I have to say?'

'Sure.'

One of the more emotional girls spoke up. 'Isn't this kind of ghoulish. Going on like this . . . ?'

Andrus suggested they take a vote. When the hands were counted most of the cast was for going ahead.

Columbo stepped out of the wings.

'Excuse me. I'm Lieutenant Columbo, Los Angeles Police Department. I wonder if I could ask you people a few questions?'

The cast of thirty-two students looked bewildered and – it seemed to Columbo – a little frightened. And why not? They had enough to be frightened about. If there were a random killer stalking the theater anyone might be a victim next. Columbo made a mental note to increase the patrol. 'I'll keep this simple,' he said. 'Anybody hear anything last night? See anything strange . . . out of the ordinary?'

The students all looked at him blankly. One or two shook their heads negatively.

'Think about it. Think about seeing anything out of place. Like that.' He coughed. Took out his notebook. 'Look. This is pretty tough on you all. I know that. You've got a lot of guts going on with your show. If you can think of anything that'll help me out in finding who did this, you can tell me. It'll be in confidence. That's a promise. That's O.K. for now.'

A voice hailed Columbo as he trudged into the wings toward the stage door. 'Lieutenant?' Turning around he saw Linda Kitteredge approaching. 'I . . . I'm Linda Kitteredge. I don't know if it means anything but Dean Borchardt always stayed late this whole week. I mean, after we all left after rehearsal he'd stay and check things out.'

'I appreciate that. Thanks.'

'It probably doesn't help, but you said if we thought of anything.'

'A lot of people knew about that?'

'We all did.'

Columbo considered that sentence a moment. His first instinct was that no student was involved with the murder, but he tended to forget that these college students weren't children. They were men and women capable of any action any adult might perform. 'If you all knew it a lot of other people knew it too?'

'I'm sure.'

'Thanks. What part do you have in this play?'

'I play Vittoria Corombona.'

'Is that a good part?'

'It's the one everything sort of spins around. She's the White Devil of the title.'

'Is that right? Title role, huh? You must be pretty good.'

'It's just a student production.'

'My wife, she thought about doing some acting once. Benefit for some organization. With her friends. But she's shy. Can't go out in front of people. Would you believe I'm a little bit that way myself. I mean, just now. Talking to all of you there . . . how many is it?'

'Thirty-two.'

'Thirty-two people like that on a stage. I had butterflies.'

'But that's your job isn't it Lieutenant?'

'I don't know if being on stage is my job. I get into some funny things. Well, thanks for the information . . .' Columbo nodded goodbye and began walking to the stage door. He hesitated a minute and turned. 'Hey, listen. Did you notice . . . did anybody notice . . . ? Did anybody else stay with him?'

'With Dean Borchardt?' Linda asked.

'Yeah. Last night.'

'I did, Lieutenant. Last night.'

'Is that right?'

'I've had some trouble with some of the more poetic lines. Pronunciation. Phrasing. I wanted to go over some of the phrasings with him before tonight.'

'So you were with him?'

'Not for long though. He had to set the lights. He told me we could do it this afternoon.'

'He do that by himself? Set the lights?'

'No. He did it with the light man, Peter.'

'Which one's he?'

'The one sitting on the crate on the far side of the stage? Very tall, with the hair in his eyes?'

'So he stayed late. I'll remember that thanks. And you just stayed a minute?'

'Resetting and double-checking light cues was more important to Mr Borchardt just then . . . It takes longer than talking over the lines.'

'It's that complicated, huh?'

'The lights set the whole mood of the production, Lieutenant.'

'I'll remember that. You know I like the theater. Real people acting and talking. I like that a lot.'

'Maybe you'll come and watch the rehearsal tonight?'

'I'll think about that. Thanks.'

Linda watched Columbo walk off and disappear through the stage door. Maybe it was foolish to volunteer information. But why not? She would cooperate all the way, and throw this little basset-hound detective completely off the scent. Things were so easy when you were young!

CHAPTER 8

Columbo felt out of place in the cool quiet wood-paneled corridors of Meredith Hall. There was a hush in the atmosphere of the administration building; the decor was probably designed to convey an air of serenity and thoughtfulness: the lush-carpeted quiet, the sweeping staircase, the oil portraits and intermittent chrystal chandeliers tended to set one a little bit on edge. If not a sacred place, at least Meredith Hall suggested a very special one separated from the world; a place where thought could flower.

The second floor administrative offices; a large suite consisting of the President's office, a central secretarial office and through a connecting door, the Dean's office, came as a relief after the silence on the main floor. Columbo found the familiar click of typewriters a welcome sound after the downstairs hush. He introduced himself to the two women trying to work: Miss Purdom and Miss Schlesinger.

Miss Schlesinger was not really working. She was obviously too distraught over her boss's death. She shuffled papers; filed away others. Sat and rose alternately from her desk chair. She sniffed continually.

Columbo glanced around the room and acquainted himself with the geography, 'The Dean worked in there?' He pointed left. 'And Mr Torrance, the President works in there?' He pointed right. Purdom confirmed. 'They work pretty well together?'

Miss Purdom answered crisply. 'As with any relationship, Lieutenant, they had their disagreements. But on the whole they enjoyed good co-ordination.'

'Would you mind if I took a look at Mr Borchardt's office?'

Schlesinger sniffed and nodded affirmatively.

The Dean's office was not what Columbo expected. It was a vast clutter of papers, file folders, books, photos, posters, tapes, newspapers and magazines. 'I try to keep it in order,' Miss Schlesinger sniffed behind Columbo. 'He is . . . was impossible, Lieutenant. His mind was such an active, searching place. It's a terrible loss.'

Columbo couldn't help but feel sorry for the woman. She had obviously been deeply devoted to her employer. 'You mind if I look around?'

'Anything. Anything at all!'

'Thanks.'

He plunged into the debris-filled room. After a moment's bewilderment he sat at the desk. The stack of papers practically obscured Columbo's view of the door. He sat in the chair gently swiveling back and forth, trying to see with Borchardt's eyes. What he saw: the piles of papers, folders, pictures, the door to the outer office bespoke an active fragmented life. A man who went from one thing to the other quickly, a restless, energetic, possibly challenging man. Probably, Columbo thought, irritating.

On the desk immediately in front of Columbo lay several neat folders marked 'Immediate', 'Correspondence', 'White Devil', 'Private'. Columbo was drawn by the 'Private' file because it was so slender. When he opened it, he found a slip of paper in it which read: 'Box'. Columbo looked around automatically for a box . . . correspondence file, shoe box, safe deposit

. . . ? What kind of box? He called Miss Schlesinger.

'Did Mr Borchardt have some kind of special place where he kept private papers?'

She thought a moment, a small lace handkerchief held in her hand. 'No, sir. Not that I know of.'

'Right.'

She continued standing in the doorway expectantly. Columbo was distracted, however. After a moment, when he became aware of her, staring at him, he told her to go.

He picked up the file marked 'Immediate'. The letters in it all awaited Borchardt's signature. The top letter was an answer (presumably) to a letter from a parent about a particular student with a physical handicap. A very kind letter, thought Columbo, carefully phrased. Borchardt was considerate of human feelings. The next several letters were routine matters having to do with a proposed student union; Columbo read the next letter in the file twice. It was addressed to the President of the Vermeer Fund and read:

Dear Vincent:

You can understand my personal disappointment in the Fund's refusal of the Indian Study Program. As I often told you this was a pet project of mine; one in which I invested a great deal of emotion to get off the ground.

In all candor, I cannot understand why the Fund turned the proposal down. I reviewed the papers time and again; I double checked them with the Bureau of Indian Affairs as well as the the indians' own more militant organizations. The figures were sound and the scale of growth over the next five years was realistic.

I urge you and your trustees not to close the books on this application just yet. For reasons I prefer discussing in person, I think the proposal was not presented in its best light and may even have been altered between the time it left my office and arrived in your hands. I am instructing my secretary to call you the week of the 15th for an appointment. I'm fully confident, Vincent, that when you hear what I have to say, you'll present the plan to your Trustees for re-evaluation.

Best personal regards,

'For reasons I prefer discussing in person . . .' the phrase echoed and re-echoed through Columbo's head. The proposal 'may have been altered' . . . hints of paranoia, or honest suspicions that someone was out to undermine the project? Whatever suspicions Borchardt had were real. Columbo had just seen his corpse carted off to the city morgue. He called Miss Schlesinger again.

Columbo stood up. 'I don't know much about this business of running a college.'

'I was just his secretary, Mr Columbo.'

'Yeah. I know that. That'll give you a little knowledge into his business. Like there's a letter there to a Vermeer Foundation . . . ?'

'He was very disappointed that they turned him down.'

'I guess so. He was fighting to get that open again. How much money was involved in a thing like that?'

'I think about one million five hundred thousand dollars.'

'Is *that* right?'

'As I remember the application, yes, Mr Columbo.'

'That's a lot of money.'

'The plan was ambitious. Dean Borchardt wanted to set up an Indian Studies Program that would service the entire southwest and provide not just an education for young indians, but an education drawn from their own history and background. He was very excited about it and very disappointed by the refusal.'

'He thought he had it in the bag?'

'Yes, sir.'

'That's a lot of money. This college business is big business?'

'I'm the wrong person to ask, Mr Columbo.' She sniffed again, audibly.

'His personal life? Wife . . . kids?'

'His wife is German. Annette. They'd had a hard time lately, but this of course hurts her terribly.'

'Hard time?'

'Dean Borchardt was a very lonely man; his work was his whole life. He considered each student his personal responsibility and he *really* cared, Lieutenant. It left him little time for a personal life. He was a blunt man, sometimes a very crude man, but everybody respected and loved him!'

Columbo was afraid that Miss Schlesinger was going to break down again. 'He had a lot of things going?' He made a gesture taking in all the papers in the room.

She attempted a smile. 'He wasn't too well organized.'

'That's a truth, Lieutenant.' Torrance stood in the door behind Miss Schlesinger. She looked around, startled. Then asked if she could leave. She escaped quickly.

'Is this the kind of police procedure you lectured the law school about, Lieutenant?'

'I guess it is, sir. Yes.'

'It'll be a pleasure watching you work. Come up with anything?'

'Too soon to tell, Mr Torrance.'

'If you're trying to work up a profile on Mr Borchardt, I can tell you this: he was a driving, ambitious man who tended to over-reach himself. He made a lot of enemies with his abrasive techniques. I found him difficult myself.'

'What about the students, sir?'

'Arnold Borchardt was one of them. In spirit. They loved him. That's one reason he could direct these yearly plays so successfully . . . come with me Lieutenant. I enjoy talking to you, but my office is somewhat more comfortable.'

Columbo followed Torrance to his office. The contrast couldn't be more severe. The only papers in view in the President's room were a few on his desk for signature. Every other surface was bare. The order perfect.

Torrance smiled: 'We were very different men, Columbo. I am well organized and, frankly, don't believe in papers or loose ends. What a man can't do in a day isn't worth doing and what he can't hold in his head isn't worth knowing.'

'I wish I was like you, sir. I'm more like Dean Borchardt there.' He fumbled in his clothes. Finally finding his notebook, he added: 'I can't ever find anything.' Columbo leafed through the notebook. 'I wanted to ask you a couple of questions.'

'By all means.'

'Last night I noticed you had some of that white powder – resin – on your shoes. Like they use on the stage?'

'You *are* observant. I'd been to the theatre, Lieutenant. I like to keep up with what's going on.'

'I was wondering, sir. It's not a usual thing and I noticed the same thing on Mr Borchardt's shoes . . .'

'Perfectly legitimate, Columbo! I hope I'm a suspect.'

'I don't understand you, sir.'

'Shouldn't everyone be a suspect until they're completely cleared?'

'It can work that way, yes.'

'Well, then. Don't play favorites.'

'You're not too high up there on the list, Mr Torrance.'

Torrance laughed. 'I'm glad to hear it, Columbo. Very glad.' With a twinkle in his eye, he added, 'And very relieved.'

'Is it true that Mr Borchardt had trouble with his wife?'

'Miss Schlesinger must have told you. Yes. But it was an odd circumstance. They were reportedly going to separate and divorce, but he never quite moved out. I think Annette was Arnold's closest friend. They couldn't make a life together, but they couldn't quite wrench it apart.'

'Just wondering.'

'If you suspect, Annette, Lieutenant, forget it. You'll see what I mean when you meet her.'

'I think there were more people involved than just one, Mr Torrance.'

Torrance took a beat on the statement. 'The coffin, huh?'

Columbo confirmed Torrance's assumption and proceeded to ask the President a series of routine questions about the operations of the University. Torrance answered with candor and good humor. A man very much at ease. Too much at ease, in fact, for the chief administrator whose right hand man had been found murdered a few hours earlier and who, as President of a University, was responsible for the safety of an entire campus.

The only time he'd even blinked was when Columbo indicated that the murder was committed by more than one person.

CHAPTER 9

Linda Kitteredge watched the sand play through her toes as she stood on the beach overlooking the Pacific Ocean. The sun, an enormous orange globe, hovered above the line of the horizon. Linda thought it looked like an immense ascension balloon and imagined the thrilling sensation as the balloon began its ascent. That would be morning of course, and not this delicious evening with its cool caressing air. In the evening the balloon sank. If she were riding the sun's gondola tonight she would descend instead of rise, entering some strange realm beyond the lip of the ocean. Then, rounding the Earth's curve she would rise again on a new morning elsewhere, in China perhaps; so that her enormous fiery balloon could rise and descend in one action: magically, like the fairy-tale voyages of childhood.

Torrance's hand on her shoulder sprung Linda from her reverie. He kissed the top of her head. 'You smell good,' he said.

'Hi. I was dreaming of riding the sun.'

'An act reserved for the Gods. All the mortals who tried it came croppers. Poor Phaeton was burned to a crisp . . . and Daedalus who flew too close to the sun with his wings made of wax plummeted to earth when the heat softened them.'

'My wings aren't wax. And, as you know, Frank, I don't melt so easily.'

'I seem to. We should stay as far apart as possible right now. If anyone sees us . . . to hell with it.'

'Take a walk?' She ran down the beach ahead of him. She was the very picture of beauty and grace, her long blonde hair flowing out behind her, the orange sun setting in the distance, the beach and the quiet roar of the gentle waves. 'It's like living in an advertisement,' Torrance thought following after her.

'Hey, come on!' Linda yelled.

'Not dressed for it,' he shouted back.

'Just stodgy!' Linda muttered when Torrance caught up with her. She took his hand. 'Look at you. Coming to the beach in dark suit and black shoes.' She laughed. 'You really are a college President!'

'I'm worried.'

'Oh, Frank!'

'This Lieutenant Columbo bothers me.'

'With his little dog face and dog manners!'

'I've had a lot of experience with people, Linda. Don't knock it. He's very, very shrewd. And he doesn't miss a trick. He knew I'd been to the theatre last night?'

'How did he do that?'

'When I saw him at the Law School reception, he noticed the resin on my shoes. Nothing had happened then and he picked up on that detail. Habit. A man with a habit of observation like that is dangerous.'

'That's pretty sharp! I like that.'

'You're not worried?'

'No!' She ran away from him again, along the breaking waves, her feet dancing in and out of the ocean foam. She seemed happy and carefree. Torrance watched her unbelievingly. She found a rock to sit on on the beach. It was big enough for two. They sat together and watched the edge of the sun's disk just touch the horizon. Then as the Pacific waters nibbled away at the large orange, and dusk replaced day, they talked, holding hands like children.

'It's very exciting,' she said.

'It's frightening, Linda. I can't believe we did it.'

'It was so easy!'

He shook his head and thought.

'They won't find us out, Frank.'

'I wish I could be sure.'

'Just play it cool. I talked to that Columbo today. I was very cooperative. You've got to figure that there's no *reason* to suspect us. You've got to act a little. I don't feel like a murderer—'

'Don't use that word . . .'

'I don't feel like I've done any harm. You're very sensitive.'

'Damn it all! Murderer's an ugly word.'

'It's an ugly thing we did. So what. God, life would be dull without that!'

Torrance stood up. 'Is it just a thrill for you? Is that all? A stupid thrill? Something to make your blood run a little faster?'

'There's damned little that does it!'

'Is that all you're about?'

'Maybe! What the hell's wrong with it? I can live the way I want.'

'Oh, God!'

He started walking back the way they had come. Several white gulls fought over a crab. A sandpiper hopped nonchalantly out of his way. Linda still sat.

He turned and looked toward her, but she continued sitting. 'I don't want to lose you,' he shouted.

He saw her head bob up and turn toward him, but

couldn't make out her expression. He felt foolish, but stood his ground, waiting.

Half the sun had dissolved before Linda joined him. 'If you think I'm such a bitch why do you even care?'

'I don't know. I wonder how I got into this whole thing. I'm fifty-seven-years-old, Linda. I'm President of a fine University. I'm respected all over the country and look – here I am carrying on with a twenty-one-year-old girl, and guilty of murdering my own Dean of Students!'

'Sounds interesting. You have any other problems?'

'You can't connect can you?'

'Oh, stodge! The world's overpopulated anyhow. One more or less . . . ?'

'That's a fine attitude.'

'So? Confess! Go on. Run down the mall at Meredith ripping off your stiff little dark suits, tearing your hair and scoring your cheeks, shouting a confession to the winds.'

He walked to the spot from where they had started their walk. She followed picking up smooth stones and shells behind him. 'I will lose you won't I?' he said.

'I don't know, Frank. I like you. We have a lot of fun together. I like that it's all secret fun and nobody knows. I love the afternoons you come over and we pull the shades. I love it when you take your clothes off and stop being Mr College President and then the next day I see you standing in front of the faculty or something looking so authoritative and debonair and establishment and they don't *know*. Only *I* know and it's exciting! But I don't like it when you start trying to hold too tight and when you're like this all uptight and afraid. I don't like it that you feel so guilty sometimes and can't just swing loose with things as they happen. I don't like it sometimes when you make a thing about the difference in our ages. I *know* how old you are. I could be your daughter. And that's interesting too because incest sounds exciting.'

'So I will lose you?'

'Ultimately. When I've had enough. When I want to go somewhere. When it's inconvenient. Yes. Why not?'

'Right? Why not?'

She took his hand. 'But not for a long time yet.'

'You're too sure of yourself, Linda.'

'Yup!'

'You'll make a mistake that way. You don't think anything through.'

'I'm not a wise graybeard.'

'Not on this Borchardt thing. Be careful. You're underestimating the enemy.'

'Columbo? Oh, Frank. He's just a funny little police lieutenant. I'll take care of him.'

'*Please!* Listen to what I'm saying!'

'I love it that you're so powerful and scared. I'm nobody.'

He kissed her cheek. 'I think I love you.'

'It's just sex. But it's fun.'

'Oh, I don't know. It sure feels good though. You're some strange exciting girl.'

'And I've got you, don't I? You're all mine.' She laughed loud and long. 'Oh, you're all mine, my darling! And you won't even argue.'

Her laughter accompanied the sun into the other world where it would rise on someone else's day. Her laughter, which was all her own frightened and thrilled Frank Torrance.

CHAPTER 10

A spare audience of about fifty stalwart friends of the production watched the house lights dim before the Act I, Scene 1 curtain went up on the Meredith Players dress rehearsal of *The White Devil.* The talking stopped. The curtain rose. Three young actors costumed in tights, capes and swords appeared in a soft orange glow of light. A single column suggested a Roman street.

LODOVICO: Banished!
ANTONELLI: It grieved me much to hear the sentence . . .

The first scene unfolded slowly, deadeningly. The actors fumbled, missed their moves across the stage. The poor fellow playing the third character in the group, Gasparo, tripped on his own sword. The audience, embarrassed for their friends, maintained a discreet, though critical, silence. The short scene was mercifully over quickly.

Horn music came up over the speakers. Stage hands dressed as seventeenth-century courtiers carried on two ornate wooden chairs; rolled out a carpet and carried on two screens painted with curlicue patterns shaped like gothic arches.

Linda, resplendent and more beautiful than ever in a metallic blue satin gown strode on to the stage attended by three male characters and two servants. One of the servants stumbled on a corner of the carpet.

Columbo, standing in the backstage shadows watched

this parade with growing interest. He understood very little of what was going on. In the first scene he had perked up at the lines:

GASPARO: You have acted certain murders here in
Rome,
Bloody and full of horror.

but if the police lieutenant was expecting the careful and logical unrolling of a murder mystery, then he was about to be cruelly disappointed. The strange old-fashioned lines seemed to tell of some kind of adulterous intrigue. Vittoria (Linda) entered and exitted. Then her brother (or so it seemed) a character in yellow tights named Flamineo, arranged for a mustachioed and bearded fellow by the name of Brachiano to hide while the brother talked a guy named Camillo out of going to bed with his own wife (Vittoria) that night. This taken care of (and cleverly, Columbo thought) Vittoria and Brachiano started passing some very hot lines back and forth full of double meanings and hinting at strange dark doings. Columbo began to understand why Camillo was removed from the scene for the evening.

The scene that had so impressed Torrance the night before continued. Vittoria suggested the murder of her husband by relating her dream. Within the context of Borchardt's death the dream took on a deeper more ominous tone. Columbo had some trouble understanding many of the old lines. But he fully understood Flamineo's observation upon those lines:

FLAMINEO: Excellent Devil! she hath taught him in a
dream
To make away his duchess and her husband!

And in the next line Brachiano affirmed it. Saying he would protect her from her jealous husband and his own jealous wife. Some doings for Italians thought Columbo! No question the play would get bloodier from here on out.

As the mayhem onstage continued, Columbo decided to explore the backstage area where he was standing. He felt that something might present itself to suggest Borchardt's killer. The difference between the ordered, if somewhat stumbling logic, onstage and the madcap chaos backstage was a surprise to him. Students were running about everywhere; the stage manager was barking orders into a small headset; the light technicians were standing at the huge board pulling levers and reading cues to each other; actors stood everywhere waiting for their entrances while costume girls pinned them and adjusted costumes; a young girl who looked no older than 10 years old, but was really 19, went about daubing make-up on sweaty, stained faces.

Linda stood directly in the left wing, waiting an entrance line. As she turned around to adjust her long skirt, she saw Columbo standing there. Their eyes met and then, much to Columbo's surprise she winked at him and walked out on to the stage.

He couldn't have said what he was looking for. He had a definite sense that things were falling apart backstage; that the rehearsal was going badly. When the young man playing Brachiano came off again he was fuming. He had blown four lines. The stage manager seemed particularly manic and hysterical. Someone muttered 'It's a mess.'

At intermission Columbo wandered into the dressing rooms. He heard universal complaints. The lights were wrong. People forgot lines. Costumes didn't fit. Music cues came in late. In short, it was worse than the ordinary terrible dress rehearsal. The men's dressing room was a-howl with protest and an attempt to pull things together for Act II. The strain of performing in the face of the day's events was clear.

The girls, of whom there were fewer, were calmer. They sat quietly, touching up their make-up, adjusting skirts and bodices, talking softly. They seemed to take their attitude from Linda, who sat silently in one corner of the women's dressing room, staring out into space. When Columbo knocked and politely introduced himself to the room, she responded with a winning smile. 'It's terrible isn't it, Lieutenant?'

'I'm no judge really. My wife—'

'Dress rehearsals are traditionally bad. The saying is that a bad dress rehearsal means a wonderful opening night.'

'I can't judge as I was telling you—'

'It's a wonderful play.'

'A lot of the words . . . they're kind of old-fashioned.'

'Jacobean . . . I love that. Did you hear my yew tree speech?'

'The one about killing somebody?'

'Indirectly, killing someone, Lieutenant. Not directly. Vittoria does nothing herself.'

'Speaking of that I was wondering a couple of things.'

'Yes?'

'Last night – you don't mind talking about this before going back on stage there?'

'Not at all, Lieutenant. It keeps my mind off all the mistakes we're making. And it's somehow in keeping with the lurid events onstage.'

'Well then . . . I checked up on some addresses . . .'

He fumbled for his notebook. 'Here. Dean Borchardt lived very near you. About a block away.'

'That seems right.'

'It seems kind of strange that you didn't walk home with him last night. Or wait to walk with him.'

'Why, lieutenant?'

'Well, you were neighbors?'

'He had the lights to worry about.'

'You don't mind walking home by yourself . . . ?'

'I always walk home by myself.'

Columbo nodded. 'Yeah.' He began to walk from the dressing room and then turned around . . . 'I always thought people in a play were kind of close.'

'It can be like a family. Sometimes.'

'If you had something to talk with him about, wouldn't you wait and take advantage of that extra time?'

'Not necessarily. Why? Several other students live on the same street, Lieutenant, why pick on me?'

'I thought . . . being the last one to see him . . . you might have noticed something.'

'I wish I could help.'

A stage hand stuck his head in the door and shouted: 'Places'.

'I have to go now.' Linda stood up. 'Are you staying for the second act?'

'I thought I'd go over and talk to Mr Torrance . . .'

'Oh!' Linda seemed disinterested as she drifted past Columbo on her way toward the stage; but he noticed a flicker of surprise; a slight thing. He was beginning to respect this girl's self-possession. She was more at ease with herself and calm around people than many older people he'd known.

CHAPTER 11

Hilda Torrance answered the door. Columbo stood waiting. She didn't believe he was a policeman until he showed his badge. Surprised, she commented 'Well. Wonders never cease!'

Columbo was struck by her grace and elegance. She wore a simple shirt-waist dress and flat casual shoes, all in varying lavender tones. She was a tall woman, who seldom wore high-heeled shoes although her husband was taller. Both towered over Columbo.

After he introduced himself, Hilda showed him into the living room. Torrance sat at a gaming table, the counters of an advancing backgammon contest arrayed on a board in front of him. Hilda announced Columbo.

'Ah, yes! Our crime fighter. Welcome. He offered Columbo a drink which was turned down. 'Do you play backgammon, Lieutenant?'

Columbo confessed that checkers were more along his line. Torrance explained that backgammon was an ancient game dating back to Ur of the Chaldees and the time of the Biblical Abraham. 'The Romans called it *ludus duodecim scriptorum*, very much like this game in front of me. It's played in the orient a great deal. The point being, I suppose, that it is fun to have some connection with the ancient past, even if it is only a diverting game.'

'That's very interesting, sir.'

'Lieutenant Columbo isn't at all interested, Frank.

He is polite.' Hilda turned to Columbo. 'You are very polite. Frank likes to show off his erudition sometimes, since he has precious little occasion to do it in his current situation.'

'Hilda would much rather be married to an abstract philosopher, than a concrete administrator!'

'Philosophers can be very witty,' she protested. 'It's somewhat mundane to find out that the academic life involves so much *business*. I would have hoped for some dedication to knowledge . . .'

'And so it goes, the ancient merry-go-round.' Torrance stood. 'I cannot offer you checkers, Lieutenant. I presume you've come for information.'

'About this appalling business with Arnold Borchardt?' Hilda added.

'Yes, ma'am. There's a lot of things troubling me about it. Very confusing.'

'What can I do?' Torrance moved to the bar and mixed himself a drink.

'Well, sir. You say Mr Borchardt had a lot of enemies. I believe that's true. I've checked around some. But it's kind of the difference between friends and acquaintances. His enemies were more like casual acquaintances than really murderous antagonists. If you see what I mean?'

'I like that comparison, Lieutenant. I'll want to remember it.'

'I'm sure that in your sensitive position, you've got a lot of people who disagree with you.'

'I'm insulated to an extent. Borchardt – deans take a lot of the heat off the President. I'm a figurehead and backroom man—'

'Like the Godfather,' Hilda interjected.

'Not quite so sinister. But I deal with the hidden

wheels until there's a real crisis, then I'm supposed to move in with my smooth and efficient expertise.'

'If I've got this right, sir. The deans, like Borchardt, handle all the problems that agitate. But when they can't handle it, you move in.'

'That's right.'

'Wouldn't your life be in danger?'

'In spite of poor Arnold's fate, Academia isn't too dangerous.'

'That's what I mean, sir. That's what I always thought.'

'Which means of course,' Hilda thought aloud, 'that Arnold was killed for some personal rather than university reason.'

'Exactly, ma'am.'

'I see your point, Columbo.' Torrance sounded gruff. He drained off what was left of his drink.

'Arnold wasn't much of a tom-catter?' She looked at her husband.

'Mr Torrance told me about the trouble with his wife.'

'She's an efficient German girl, Columbo. I think the two of them were mismatched.' Hilda had taken over answering the questions, while Torrance looked on. 'Arnold needed someone to roll his socks and keep dinner on the back burner till he came home. Annette . . . well . . . Annette is not that person. She is unhappy in the United States . . . she would like to have some little business of her own . . . she's very good with her hands. She makes things . . . you'll see. I have to say, for Arnold, he understood her. But he was too busy helping himself to help her.'

'I guess he didn't have regular hours, huh?'

'No Lieutenant. None of them do.' She turned to

Torrance. 'The man you see here is spending his first full evening at home in six months.'

'That's an exaggeration, Hilda?'

She merely shrugged. Columbo felt uncomfortable, stuck suddenly in the middle of a domestic quarrel.

Torrance broke the growing silence. 'There's a lot of night-time activity in a university, Lieutenant. Hilda has never reconciled herself to my taking such an active interest.'

'Well, sir, I'm sure that's correct. I just came from the theater myself and on my way I saw lights on in a lot of lecture halls. It's very impressive.'

'You were at the dress rehearsal, were you, Lieutenant?'

'Those kids have a lot of guts putting that play on today like that.'

'Yes, they do.'

'The show must go on.' Hilda shot a terrible look at Torrance, and left the room.

Torrance manoeuvered Columbo to the door. 'Anything more I can do, you'll come to me, Lieutenant?'

'Yes, sir. I will. Thank you.'

The moment the door closed behind the detective, Hilda stormed out again. 'What do you know about Arnold's murder, Frank?'

'No more than anyone else. Why so fierce, Hilda? Just because you're losing at backgammon?'

'This isn't funny.'

'You heard what I said to Columbo?'

'I began to put two and two together. This morning, when you were so pensive about dying and concocted your very romantic plan to meet in Europe—'

'I told you about an old college chum who'd dropped dead on the street!'

'Frank, you didn't know about Arnold before anyone else?'

'Hilda!'

'You were too mellow this morning. I was sure something had frightened you.'

'I was frightened. But about death from natural causes.' Torrance tried to take Hilda into his arms. 'I just don't feel quite so invulnerable as I used to.'

She allowed him to hold her. 'I know you *very* well, Frank Torrance! Something's bothering you. Something way down there . . . I'll find out what it is. Sooner or later I'll know—'

'Don't be so smug.' He kissed her. And kissed her again.

As he drove through the university grounds, Columbo thought about his visit with the Torrances. He had entered a room brim full of warmth and domestic quiet and left behind one trembling with tension. Hilda Torrance's quip about her husband being home for the first time in six months was no idle joke. Why first of all was he away from home so much? And why was he home tonight of all nights? Was there a connection with the extraordinary events of the day? Torrance knew a little more than he was telling. That seemed certain. Somewhere there was a tension between Borchardt and an unknown that resulted in murder. Was it Annette Borchardt? Did she have a lover? Did she resent her husband hanging on after he'd made the decision to leave? How much did the President know about this conflict? And why wasn't he telling? Concerned with the image of the university in the public mind, was he hiding something that could be fundamentally damaging to the university in the future? Or was *he* that unknown? Was he the one Borchardt was in conflict with?

A neon sign flashed 'Ellen's University Spoon'. Hungry, Columbo pulled his old car into a parking space and entered the warmly-lighted and colorfully-decorated shop. In spite of the late hour the place was crowded, populated by bleary-eyed students scruffy in uniform of the day: jeans, work shirts, loose sweaters. The steady hum of conversation was pleasing and restful.

Columbo slipped on to a stool between two long-haired undergraduates, and ordered a bowl of chili. As he methodically spooned food into his mouth, he realized he needed a better view of the relationships within the administration. It wasn't unreasonable to think that if (a) Borchardt was having an administrative conflict and (b) Torrance was holding something back there might be a relation between (a) and (b). Columbo nodded. 'You a student here?' The detective turned to a dark-haired abstracted young man in metal-rimmed glasses to his left. The boy nodded sullenly. 'You like it?' The boy nodded again. 'Yeah,' Columbo spooned. 'You study something particular?' Again the fellow nodded affirmatively, and continued eating scrambled eggs. 'You know anything about the administration? President Torrance? Dean Borchardt?'

The boy turned to Columbo. 'Borchardt's dead.' He looked critically at Columbo. 'You the murderer?'

'Police.' Columbo fumbled for his badge and showed it to the young man.

'A lot of good that'll do.'

'We've got to try.'

'You're wasting your time around here. It was an outside job.'

'Outside job?'

'Some crazy went in the back door of the theatre, probably too stoned or something and totaled the first guy that got in his way. It happened to be Dean Borchardt.'

'That's a theory all right.'

'So you'll never find who did it.'

'What did you think of Mr Borchardt?'

'He was the best goddamn dean this place ever had. He was one of us. He dug the students. Understand. He grooved on our circuits. His vibes were right in there...'

Columbo ruminated over his chili a minute. Torrance had been at pains to describe Borchardt's enemies. And here he was praised to the skies by the only constituents that really counted. His students. Columbo turned to his right. The boy there was half asleep and humming to himself, bobbing a huge head of curly hair to some kind of inner rhythm. 'What did you think of Dean Borchardt?'

The eyes sprung wide. 'A very great human being!'

Columbo turned to the first student. 'You have any thoughts about President Torrance?'

'Mr Ice. He doesn't exist and he doesn't know we exist.'

'Well, of course he's got a lot of duties . . .'

'He's outside the whole sphere. Outer space. Gone. Too far away. Who is he anyhow?' He leaned across Columbo to address the curly-haired student: 'Do you know anybody name of Torrance?'

'What's that? A lost planet?'

Columbo got the message.

Annette Borchardt proved to be a tiny compact brunette; not the Juno-esque Germanic type Columbo had been led to expect. She was as composed in her emotions as she was, economically structured physically. The only mark of grief or disappointment she bore was the trim black suit she was wearing. Her face was composed, her eyes calm.

The Borchardt home reflected the wife. Neat, tidy, old world. A few antiques here and there; an oriental carpet; some porcelains in cabinets, lace on the chairs. Everything in order. A sharp contrast from her husband's paper-strewn office.

Another woman, somewhat older than Annette sat in a straight-backed wing chair in the living room. She was introduced as a close friend kind enough to stay the night with Annette. Columbo was introduced as a police officer. The other woman nodded tightly. Columbo cleared his throat. He felt like Edgar the Elephant with two left feet.

'I hate to bother you at a time like this . . . but I've got to ask just a couple of questions.'

'Quite appropriate.' She spoke with the slightest German accent. If Columbo hadn't known better he would have guessed she was British.

'This is an unfortunate time . . .' Columbo cleared his throat. 'Did your husband ever mention any people who might be out to hurt him for some reason?'

'Hurt, Arnold? Why should Arnold be hurt?'

'You know, in the line of business? Things come up. Some people get a little wild sometimes. Was he afraid of anything?'

'Arnold never spoke to me of anything to be afraid of. No!'

'He worked pretty hard?'

'Yes.'

'Did he discuss his work with you at all, Mrs Borchardt?'

'No. Very little. We . . . were not on the best of terms, Lieutenant. The last days. We had talked about divorce in fact, though this was commonly known.'

'You've got to excuse this next question. Was there another man? Or another woman in either of your lives?'

'No. We just realized we were not suited to one another. It happens often enough.'

'And there was no trouble about the divorce?'

'No. Arnold was going to take care of it during the intersession.'

'Was he still coming home nights?'

'Yes. He did not want to leave me, he said, until the last minute.'

'How did you feel about that, ma'am?'

'I respected him. During this time of his play he was, of course, always late.'

'And when the play wasn't taking his time?'

'Arnold liked always to be home for dinner. He enjoyed my cooking.'

'It doesn't seem like you had much reason to separate.'

Annette's hands, tightly folded in her lap, gripped themselves tighter and tighter. She was under extreme tension. She wasn't as emotionally controlled as she was shy, Columbo decided. 'Yes. It looks strange. Arnold was . . . I could not fulfil myself in Arnold's shadow. He understood. He was too busy with himself. But we were good friends.'

Columbo stood. 'I'm sorry I had to bother you ma'am. You're sure that's the only reason you were divorcing?'

She nodded affirmatively.

At the door, Annette spoke. 'Lieutenant. I want you to get the man who did this terrible thing. Arnold was a very good and valuable man. I loved him once and I never lost my respect for him. In our whole life together, he was always kindly. People like that must not be killed. I want this killer caught and punished, you understand? And I will do anything, anything at all to see that it happens!'

She opened the door and Columbo went out into the warm night. He drove to the theatre, his mind spinning with conflicting thoughts. His picture of Borchardt was changing hour-to-hour. Now it seemed that there was *no* motive for Arnold Borchardt's death. He was an esteemed and respected man. Some even loved him. And if even the wife who wanted a divorce still respected him then . . . then the murder became more malicious than it had seemed before. Maybe the student at the restaurant was right. Maybe this was one of those crazy, motiveless accidents where someone wandered in off the street and killed. Columbo had seen it happen before.

He returned to the theater just as most of the cast was leaving. He saw the students shuffling away from the brightly lighted building. They were not communicating with one another. They were all glum.

When Columbo entered through the stage door, he discovered why everyone was so depressed. The dress rehearsal, which they'd considered a tribute to the dead director had continued in the same disastrous fashion as it had begun. The crew tidying up, the technicians readjusting lights, the assistant director standing in the middle of the stage with his clipboard in his hands, each of them looked like they had just lived through the end of the world.

A few students were still in the dressing rooms changing clothes and tidying up. Columbo noticed the different compacts of make-up on the long table and picked one up. One of the actors told him to put it down.

'That's important, huh?'

'Each actor has his own stuff, Lieutenant. Don't mix it up.'

'How come?'

The actor seemed relieved to talk to someone outside the production. 'Everyone's got a different skin tone. Takes the light differently. Also the lights have different colored lenses on them so that the actor's got to be made up in a way that he interacts with the light.'

A few of the straggling actors wandered in, along with several actresses. Linda Kitteredge, brushing out her long hair wandered into the dressing room with them.

'Here. I'll show you,' said the actor. 'Give me your hands?'

'My hands?'

Linda Kitteredge laughed. 'Go ahead, Lieutenant. Artie won't bite.'

Columbo held his hands out. 'Now watch.' Artie took a small sponge and daubed pancake make-up on the back of Columbo's right hand. He put a different color on the left. 'See the difference?'

'Yeah.' His mind flashed back to the Law School reception the night before. The color on Torrance's cheek was lighter, pinker. 'How many different colors are there?'

'Dozens.'

'But they're all skin colors like these here?'

'No. Any color you want. Blue. Lavender. White. Red.'

'How about rosy pink?'

'Very common, Lieutenant. Most of the girls wear it. Especially those who're supposed to have an irresistible complexion.'

'That's very interesting.' He turned on the stool in front of the long table with its mirror running the length of the room. 'You girls know all about this?'

'We're actresses, Lieutenant.' Linda spoke.

'I can see why you like this so much. It's kind of fun.'

'It was fun until Dean Borchardt was killed.' One of the darker girls this time.

'Yeah. I guess it didn't go too well tonight.'

'It was a disaster. Everything went wrong that could go wrong.'

'I've been hearing a lot of theories about Mr Borchardt's death. Any of you have any ideas?'

The conversation became relaxed. About ten students were in the room now, sitting around Columbo who stayed at the dressing table. Linda Kitteredge drifted back to a far corner where she dropped on to a broken old sofa. She listened as intently to the conversation as Columbo did.

The students were not without a theory. Most thought some outsider had committed the crime; but several felt that it might be Borchardt's wife or some dark stranger from his past. One even felt it might be one of the student demonstrators whom Borchardt expelled during the 1968 riots. The particular demonstrator under suspicion had gone underground soon after it was discovered that she had been involved with illegal bomb-manufacture. She had never been found and, theorized the student, she had begun a vendetta against all those who had been in any way responsible for her outlaw status.

The students then began pressing Columbo for *his* theories. What was he thinking? But he cagily avoided their questions. He didn't want to commit the department . . .

They laughed at him. Was he an establishment lieutenant?

He had to admit he was. And also, he had to admit that he was pretty confused himself about the thing. He shook his head and muttered, 'I can't find a motive, see. When you find the motive you've got the killer. But without it . . .' He looked up and caught Linda's eyes. A small smile creased her lips. 'What do you think, Miss Kitteredge? You got any ideas on this thing?'

'Oh, I think everyone's said enough.'

'You were the next-to-last person to be with him. Didn't you see anything odd around the theater?'

'I've already told you Lieutenant. I left him adjusting lights.'

'I talked to the lighting guy. He says when he left, Borchardt was still here. He also said he thought somebody was sitting in the wings, but left anyhow. That Mr Borchardt was going to do something about the costumes. My guess is that he went back into the wings there and the killer was waiting, as the light man said. A couple of things occurred to me. One is that the killer might be anybody involved with the production, who just didn't leave. You know? Waited until the theatre was empty. And the other thing bothering me is that I think I'm looking for two people instead of one.'

These last two statements sent a shock through the students. Linda didn't move. Someone asked 'Why?'

'Well the first thing's pretty obvious. The second is: I don't think anybody could've gotten such a bulky guy into that coffin by themselves. That took two people.'

'That blows just about everything sky high?'

'What two people . . . ?'

Columbo stood up. 'That's the problem. See.' He looked darkly around the room. 'I don't want to scare you all, but whoever they were could be in the cast.'

Everyone began to look at one another. Each protested that that was crazy. They were a great group. Students weren't murderers. In fact, Columbo noticed, everyone had something to say on that point except the girl who played the White Devil, Linda Kitteredge. She sat in her removed corner, a mysterious half-smile on her lips.

After the impromptu rap session, Columbo drove along the route Borchardt would have followed were he walking home. Near Borchardt's house, he spotted Linda Kitteredge, her long hair in a relaxed fall below her neck and shoulders. Columbo pulled up beside her.

'Want a lift?'

'Why not?' She jumped into the car next to the detective. 'Following me, Lieutenant?'

'I was just cruising along here, see if there was anything to see.'

'Like what?'

'Somebody hanging around. Somebody who shouldn't be there.'

'You mean the killer returning to the scene of the crime?'

'It's a terrible emotional thing to kill someone. People come apart in funny ways. You've got to look for that.'

'You sure you weren't looking for me?'

'I remembered you walked this way. But I wasn't looking for you. I still think it's funny you didn't walk home with him . . .'

'Aside from the fact that he had more work to do in the theater, is the fact that students and faculty shouldn't fraternize too much on a potentially sexual basis.'

Columbo gulped hard. 'I wasn't saying anything about *that* – just friends, working together. Students and faculty are friends aren't they?'

'Yes, but what I mean, Lieutenant, is that everybody knew about Dean Borchardt's marriage. And I'll be damned if I open myself to gossip with a man like that. Here's where I live.'

Columbo pulled the car to a halt in front of an absolutely tiny stucco house. 'You can't have much room in there?'

'Enough. I like it. Come in for a cup of coffee?'

'I don't want anybody starting any rumors about us . . . you know . . . ?' Columbo smiled slyly. 'My wife . . . she's very jealous. I come in all sorts of strange hours.'

'I won't seduce you, Lieutenant, I promise.' Linda opened the car door. 'There's always coffee, though.'

'Yeah, well. It sounds all right.' Columbo jumped out of the car and looked around carefully.

The house which was hemmed in between two larger houses consisted of a living room, a bedroom and a small kitchen. Linda explained that it used to be a garage, which someone made over like this into a very cozy little place. She felt lucky to rent it.

Inside, it was decorated in a very pleasant and sophisticated manner. The furniture was all straw and vinyl. Japanese straw mats covered the floor. The curtains were very simple bolts of organdy sewn straight and hanging like orange parentheses around the windows.

Linda's books were scattered everywhere.

Columbo was struck by the neat sophistication of the place. It didn't look like a student's apartment at all. Clean upholstered furniture. A permanent look; more like the home of an independent working girl. 'I work at my studies, Columbo. What do you expect? Posters and cast-away furniture and beer cans all over?' She laughed, cheerily. 'You're from another century.'

Columbo had to admit that he was learning a great deal about modern students. Even so he wondered why she lived off campus.

'I like it. I can afford it. I'm really not too fond of other students.' She served the coffee. 'Most of them are childish and immature. In fact, Lieutenant. I rather prefer older men. And to be honest, older men don't like to follow girls home to a dormitory. Here I can lead the life I choose.'

'Privacy, huh?'

'Extreme.' She smiled.

'You like older guys like Mr Borchardt?'

'I thought I made it clear that we never had an affair. He never indicated he wanted one and I surely did not want one with him!'

'You study anything special?'

'Biology and pre-med. I might become a doctor. If I become anything.'

'That right?'

'It's interesting. I was wondering about Dean Borchardt's condition in the coffin? He died of suffocation?'

'You know that, huh?'

'I wondered.'

'It wasn't pretty. He fought pretty hard.'

'Interesting.' She took a sip of coffee.

'You didn't like him very much?'

'He was too much one of the gang for me.'

'What kind of guy do you like?'

Linda smiled teasingly. 'Are you having aggressive thoughts?'

'I've got a wonderful wife.'

'That's more than most men say. They're all unhappy with their wives, at least when they talk to me.'

'You like older men?'

'Yes. Boys . . . students . . . are a bore. All their rah-rah school days. I like men with some achievement behind them, who are someplace and don't have to work to get there. Let *their* wives suffer all that business of early struggle and failure. Life's too short: my men have arrived or to hell with them.'

Columbo was shocked again. 'Dean Borchardt was pretty prominent.'

'He was a wonderful student director. But he didn't have what it takes to make it to the top.'

'What's that?'

'Style. He had the style of a rhinoceros. Lumbering. People should have grace . . . boldness . . . oh . . . you don't want to know, Lieutenant.'

'No. That's very interesting. Is President Torrance a guy with style?'

'President Torrance?' She laughed. 'He's just an administrator.'

'Yeah.' Columbo paused to think. 'I was going to ask your opinion on something . . . but . . .'

'Ask. I'll have an opinion. I promise you.'

'It has to do with President Torrance and this murder.'

'Really! That's too bizarre, Lieutenant.'

'You seem a judge of men. Obviously you don't have much of an opinion about Mr Torrance.' He stood up to leave. 'I've been thinking he knows more than he's telling me.'

'You think that stick-in-the-mud did it?'

'No, Miss Kitteredge. I don't.'

She laughed again. 'Frank Torrance wouldn't get near anything where he'd dirty his hands.'

'I tell you it's hard to find which way to go on this.'

'I'd like to help.'

'If you remember anything about last night, you tell me.'

'I promise.'

Columbo excused himself and left.

Afterwards, it troubled Linda that he had never touched his coffee.

CHAPTER 12

High noon on the Meredith Campus. Chapel bells rang across the open lawns and over the palm trees; across the stucco buildings and dormitories; across roadways and bicycle paths, over Meredith Hall, the theater, the lecture halls and laboratories, the dormitories and playing fields. They tolled a tribute to the slain dean.

Frank Torrance stood on the stairs leading into the large moorish style interdenominational church building. He was engaged in earnest conversation with several men in dark suits. Much to his astonishment students crowded the steps and were still streaming along the paths. Even though the service had been scheduled to begin on the dot of noon. It was rare that anyone attended memorial services, but this outpouring of affection and respect for Arnold Borchardt represented an honest tribute. Torrance felt a pang of jealousy. No students would turn out for him in such large numbers.

A midnight blue Ford Torino pulled up at the curb near the church. Annette Borchardt, alone, left the car and walked toward the chapel. Noticing her, Torrance, left the men he was talking to and bounded down the steps to greet the widow. Taking her gently by the arm he began talking quietly.

She wore a trim dark suit and a dark hat with veil. Her calm was so great that she seemed hypnotized. Numb.

Torrance walked her through the crowd on the steps

and into the chapel. When these two had entered the others followed; the dark-suited gentlemen, the brightly-clothed students, hushed, two-by-two, in quiet orderly impromptu march following the University president and the dead man's widow.

When Columbo arrived a few minutes later the steps and lawns were deserted. To the accompaniment of the organ playing 'Nearer My God to Thee', Columbo hurried inside.

He too was startled by the size of the turnout. The chapel was almost full; the early afternoon sun streamed through the high windows illuminating a dazzling motley congregation listening silently to the organ. The casket stood, closed, in front of the altar. Frank Torrance sat to the left of it, next to the college minister, Reginald Kobin. When the hymn ended Kobin stood and read a prayer.

Columbo noticed that Mrs Borchardt sat in the first pew next to Hilda Torrance. Several men, whom he guessed to be faculty sat in the pews behind her. A group of older men, in dark suits, sat across the aisle from her. Spotting an empty space next to Miss Purdom, Columbo slipped into it. 'Who are those guys in the dark suits?'

'Trustees!' she whispered back to him. 'Show some respect, Lieutenant.'

'Sorry.'

Miss Schlesinger tears streaming down her face sat next to Miss Purdom.

Torrance stood.

'Excuse me.' Columbo slipped out of his seat and walked to the back of the sanctuary. He found the door leading to the stairs to the organ loft. Upstairs, he looked down on the congregation:

Torrance was speaking: '. . . humanity. Five years ago, when a judicious light touch was needed to . . .'

Columbo turned a corner in the gallery and startled the organist, a young music major. He put his fingers to his lips and showed the young man his badge. The young man nodded and Columbo followed the gallery around another corner and down its length to a position above the congregation and in front of it, where he could see everyone head on. Standing in the shadow of a doorway, Columbo himself could not be seen.

'. . . sent the police away and in an act of true courage entered the building himself . . . the results are legend. But the effect his actions had on me, personally, are not so well known. Arnold Borchardt changed my life . . .'

Carefully, systematically, Columbo scanned the faces below him. He had some vague hope that somehow the killer (if he were there in fact) would identify himself. He moved his eyes over row after row. Annette Borchardt and Hilda Torrance, faculty, trustees, students, older women who must have been secretaries and administrative staff; more students left and right. Many of the girls were crying; the young men looked miserable. Columbo recognized the faces of some of the cast members of *The White Devil*, somber sad children.

When he saw Linda Kitteredge, he was startled. He looked a second time. There was no question that the girl was smiling, ever so slightly, quietly to herself, as though she were enjoying a private joke. The same Mona Lisa smile he'd noticed last night during his rap session with the student actors.

The organ struck up a funeral march as Torrance left the altar and walked up the aisle out of the church. Hilda and Annette followed. When Torrance passed Linda's pew she winked at him.

But Columbo had already left his post in the gallery and started on his own way down and out of the chapel.

Outside now small groups formed, a buzz of conversation rose; people waited their turn to pay condolences to Annette. Torrance was surrounded by faculty, Hilda by some wives. The students generally remained apart or began drifting to their various appointments. The trustees clumped together.

Columbo approached Torrance, excusing himself to the cluster around the President. He asked to talk to him alone.

Standing apart, Columbo hummed-and-hawed a bit, scratched his head and then asked Torrance what he knew of a student named Linda Kitteredge?

Torrance didn't bat an eye. 'Linda Kitteredge? It's hard to keep track of them all, Columbo, but I think she's playing the lead in Borchardt's play.'

'Yes, sir. Well, I was curious because she was almost the last person to be with Dean Borchardt except the lighting man and I'll be checking him out myself.'

'You're free to check all the student records, Lieutenant.'

'I might have to do that. But that's some chore.'

'All of them, yes.'

'You don't have some special knowledge of this Kitteredge girl?'

'None at all. Why?'

'I thought you might have some . . . because of her . . . well, visibility, in the play and everything.'

'The generations come and go.'

Columbo drifted over and talked to some trustees as Torrance joined the group he had been with. The crowd was thinning now. The casket had been carried out a side door of the church and taken to the funeral home in a hearse.

The trustees stood saying the things one would expect of them: five men in dark suits standing together deploring the bad public relations and frightening reputation this kind of thing can have on the general public. Columbo interrupted, and when five pairs of eyes stared at him suspiciously, he presented his badge. He asked some discreet questions: their opinion of Borchardt? How effective he was? Could they think of anyone who might have wanted to murder the man? Praise for Torrance's fine eulogy. Small talk really. But Columbo couldn't help noticing Torrance watching carefully – like a hawk – as the detective talked to the trustees – for the first time since he'd been in contact with the man, Columbo saw Torrance agitated.

Columbo thanked the men for their time and returned to Torrance.

'Did you have a good talk with the bosses, Columbo?' His voice shook slightly.

'Interesting guys. They know a lot about what's going on here.'

'Are you implying anything, Columbo?'

'Oh, they speak very highly of you, sir. But they seemed to know that Mr Borchardt didn't share their opinion.'

'Come on Columbo. Don't listen to every little bit of gossip that goes around. Ever since Borchardt was appointed to office, the rumor's been going on that he and I were cut-throat enemies. It's so much nonsense. We respected each other.'

'Oh, you can take it easy on that score. Nobody mentioned anything like that at all.'

Torrance suddenly realized that Columbo had

tricked a small admission of tension from him. 'Damn,' he thought. 'I'm right about this man. Linda is too young and cocky. I've got to warn her.' Aloud, he said, 'You know there are always malicious gossips that'll spread bad news about you – especially when you're as visible as I am. It's a price of prominence.'

'I understand that, sir.'

'Have you made any progress, Lieutenant?' Torrance was trying to turn the tables. 'Any *real* progress?'

'Nothing much to talk about. Though I'm pretty sure now that Mr Borchardt was killed for personal reasons. I've counted the random killer theory out.'

'There were severe student cabals in the late sixties. Some of these kids are still at large. For bombing . . . ?'

'That's something to think about. Excuse me . . .' Columbo began moving away. The crowd had dispersed. He turned back to Torrance. 'One thing . . . bothers me. You were there that night . . . at the theater?'

'Yes, Lieutenant. I've explained that.'

'The resin . . . I understand that . . . sir. But I noticed you also had a spot of make-up on your chin . . . here . . .' Columbo indicated on his own cheek where he had seen the make-up . . .

'Make-up. Lieutenant?' Torrance laughed. I've been accused of a lot of things in my life, but making up . . . ?'

'Not woman's stuff sir . . . Stage make-up . . . like somebody might have rubbed it off on you or something. I'm sure it's nothing.'

'Oh, that!' Torrance laughed again, but forced. 'I was fooling around backstage with all those pancake make-ups the kids use. Some of it must have come off on me.'

'Was that in the men's dressing room?'

'Of course.'

'I was there myself. Doing the same thing.'

'Then you know. You must be more careful than I am.'

'I'll check the mirror in the car. It'd be hard to explain to my wife.'

'Right. Well, if that's all Lieutenant. I should get back to my office.'

'Yes, sir. Thank you.'

Torrance turned on his heel and strode off across the campus.

Columbo thought about this second lie. What Columbo had spotted on Torrance's chin had been very pink, feminine, the kind of pancake only the actresses used. The particular color was not kept on the men's make-up table.

When Columbo approached his car in the parking lot behind the chapel, he spotted Mrs Torrance sitting behind the wheel of her car. Another woman, gray-haired, short, a bit on the plump side was walking away from her. Hilda started her engine before she saw Columbo bounding across the asphalt.

'Lieutenant Columbo! How thoughtful of you to come to the memorial service. That's very decent really.'

'It wasn't all charity ma'am.'

'I'm sure you were looking – as detectives must – for clues. Have you found any?'

'Not much, no.'

'I'm sure you will.'

'Little bits and pieces.'

'I know what you mean. It *is* bizarre isn't it. Though I must say, in many ways Arnold Borchardt had it coming.'

'I get a lot of conflicting things on that.'

'I'm sure you get straight division between facult and students. From our side . . . administration an faculty . . . he was a somewhat smarmy climber. Usin his fatuous appreciation of the students to move himse into high academic position. He was terribly ambitious He didn't care whose body he climbed over . . .'

'I take it that includes your husband?'

'Oh, I'm sure he would have liked to remove Frank. Noting Columbo's expression she added, 'But I'n equally sure that Frank would never remove Arnold Oh, Lieutenant. Absurd!'

'I wasn't implying that ma'am. It's just hard to ge to the bottom of this.'

'What motive would Frank possibly have? Arnol was his junior. Frank can hardly be removed unless h does something outrageous.'

'I don't want to imply anything like that, Mr Torrance.'

'I hope not!'

'You understand I've got to think of everything?'

'Yes, I understand.' But her tone was definitel colder than before.

'There're as many possibilities as there are students Though I guess I could narrow it to the ones in the play Do you hear much about the students, Mrs Torrance?'

'Not much, no.'

'Boy things have changed since I was in college.'

'For all of us, Lieutenant.'

'Hard to keep up . . . I'm keeping you though. I'm sorry.'

'It's all right, Lieutenant. Anything to help.'

'I'm just thinking aloud kind of, but . . . wait . . .' H pulled out his notebook and fumbled through the pages, 'You ever hear of a girl named Linda Kitter-edge?'

'No . . . why?'

'She was one of the last people to be with Mr Borchardt before he was killed.'

'The name isn't familiar.'

'Yeah . . . well . . . thanks.' He shook his head negatively, discouraged – still holding the notebook.

'If that will be all, Lieutenant?'

'Yeah . . . sorry to keep you. So long.'

She released the brake and drove off leaving Columbo standing in the middle of the parking lot.

Peter Arminski wasn't in his dormitory room: a jumble of dissected radios, circuitry, tubes, light bulbs, even a pin ball machine cluttered every space except the bed and one oddly clean table top. But Arminski was not amid the clutter.

While Columbo stood in the doorway scratching his head, another student happened by, a tall skinny young man with an enormous jutting adams' apple. 'Looking for Armi? – Arminski?'

'That's right.'

'Physics lab., Hermitage Hall, Lab. 4. Every day at three o'clock.'

The tall student disappeared down the hall as Columbo was thanking him.

Peter Arminski, red hair falling all over his face, peered through a series of complex lenses at another series of complex lenses. Other students were engaged in equally odd activity: one was doing complex things with iron filings, and magnets while another was taking what looked like a group of measurements from a pendulum. Columbo strolled from one to the other, like an onlooker at a sideshow, fascinated by the devices. Arminski was in a world of his own and it took Columbo several minutes to establish his presence and even then the student just said, 'I'll be with you in a minute.' He dashed to the far end of the table to another set of lenses which he peered through for a good five minutes before squinting a look at Columbo.

'You're a cop.'

'Right.'

'I don't know anything.'

'Just checking. I've got to check everybody.'

'I appreciate thoroughness.'

'Uh . . . what're you doing here?' Columbo waved a hand toward the lense device.

'We-ell . . . this is going to be a laser experiment. Right now I'm trying out all sorts of lense alignments both concave and convex in an attempt to find a better ratio for projecting the laser beam which we're going to use to transmit sound waves. Sound transmitted by light is what it will all boil down to Lieutenant.'

Columbo bobbed. 'If that's what you say? That's really quite some-thing. You can do that?'

'These lasers are magnificent. Drill a hole through the toughest metal in a blink of an eye.'

'Kill somebody?'

'Easy. Death ray! Zap!'

Columbo smiled uneasily. 'You were the last person, I think, to be with Dean Borchardt before he was killed.'

'Not strictly true, Lieutenant. Somebody else was there when I left. I noticed a minor displacement of light in the wings near the stage door as I was going out. Somebody was back there waiting for him.'

'You're sure of that?'

'Oh, yes. I'm sensitive to light. Light and sound . . .

especially light, and I know shadows. That's why I like doing the stage lighting; it's for the shadows.'

'You didn't think that was strange?'

'Why?'

Columbo looked blank. 'The man was murdered!'

'It never happened before; people always hang around. Students find theaters like surrogate homes, Lieutenant. They're always loath to leave them. I never want to go back to my room. That place is fun.'

'Who was it, do you think?'

'In the shadows? I don't know . . . from what I remember of the light someone pretty slender. A girl maybe?'

'You can really tell that?'

'Oh, sure. You can get a pretty good idea of bulk from shadow and light displacement.'

'Did Miss Kittcredge talk to Dean Borchardt before he started in with you?'

'Yes, sir. Then she left.'

'Where'd you go from the theater?'

'Back to my room. I had a German paper to write.'

'Anybody see you?'

'Am I a suspect?'

Columbo shrugged non-commitally.

'I'd be glad to submit to a lie detector test. I've never tried a polygraph. I'd be interested to see how it worked.'

'No. That's all right for now. You'll be at the theater tonight?'

'It's opening night, Lieutenant. You bet . . .'

The boy couldn't be less interested in the investigation. He turned back to his lenses. Columbo left the lab. slowly – fascinated by all the experiments. And mulling Peter Arminski over in his mind—

CHAPTER 13

Columbo sat on a large carton in Borchardt's office, with piles of files around him. He was dusty and discouraged. He had been going steadily, carefully, tediously through the Dean's files. Now, he sat back, looked around him with despair and took out a cigar. The moment after he lit it, Miss Schlesinger materialized. Her nose, permanently red, from crying.

She stared at Columbo and the smoke rising through the air. 'The Dean did not smoke.'

Columbo merely nodded pursed his lips and took another tasty puff.

'Did you find anything, Lieutenant?'

'I was just thinking about that, Miss Schlesinger. Funny how you can go around and around on a thing like this. It comes down to going around enough times to see where the merry-go-round stops regularly. You know what I mean.'

'No, sir. But then Dean Borchardt had a way of talking in riddles.'

'His letters seem to leave a lot out of them.'

'He was very careful.'

'Yeah. Like a politician.'

'Oh! He was a very good man!'

'He was looking for another job, huh?'

'Yes, sir.'

Columbo thought. Every place he'd looked for a new appointment had turned him down. But there was something about the rejection letters that Columbo couldn't get a handle on. 'I want to read you something.'

'Yes, sir.'

He took up a file and opened it. 'It says here, "Millard Fillmore College . . ." '

Miss Schlesinger nodded.

Columbo continued: ' "Dear Dean Borchardt. We want to thank you again for your application for President of the college." ' Columbo looked up. 'That's all right.' He continued reading: ' "After a thorough review of your credentials and references, we must regrettably inform you that your application is rejected." Then the thing is signed and there's a p.s. in handwriting. "Arnold: I'm sorry I got you into this. But I thought you'd be a shoo-in. You should have been. The knife came from your own people. Better review your tracks. Let's still be friends." And so on and so on . . .'

'That was his old friend, Harvey Mergle. They went to school together and Professor Mergle was on the search committee at Fillmore.'

'Yeah. But there's something bothering me. Here's another . . . regrets and all that and then this line: "After our initial consideration and what we honestly want you to know was an excellent interview, information reached us that precludes your taking over the position at this time." What kind of information?'

'I don't know Lieutenant.'

Columbo stood up. 'I think I'll go pay Mrs Borchardt a visit. You take care of yourself.'

'Can I put all this away?'

'Go ahead. It's not doing me much good.'

*

Annette Borchardt answered the door wearing a red dress with demure white collar. She looked much better in red than in black. She was a woman who's petite size and serene countenance grew more attractive each time one saw her – the first impression was of a pinched, homely woman. But she was pretty in a delicate way. Her composure was something that Columbo had difficulty getting used to. It was not so much a chill that she exuded but she seemed surrounded by an invisible wall which could not be pierced. He understood why Borchardt, who from all accounts was a warm, effusive, fully-expressive man, might have found life with Annette ultimately difficult. She was not a woman who gave much, or sent out many sparks. She was completely wrapped in herself in what she was and so seemed mysterious, removed, a great untouchable.

She greeted Columbo appropriately.

She was alone, the friend no longer with her. Materials for decoupage were arrayed on a table in the living room: neat stacks of colored papers, a large pot of glue on a sterno-burner, several tin lunch boxes. A smock hung over a chair.

Columbo wanted to know if Borchardt had an office at home. He did not, but he did have a desk in the bedroom.

Annette showed Columbo into a room as tidy as herself. A large double-bed occupied most of the space; frilly swiss polka-dotted curtains and an oaken desk completed the furnishings.

Annette excused herself telling Columbo to help himself to whatever he needed. There was no question in his mind that Annette was totally innocent of every crime. She was open, cooperative and without any traces of fear. He ascribed her quiet to grief, a grief that was to be dealt with in the same efficient and disciplined manner as her other emotions. The woman was too orderly which made Columbo, perpetually crumpled, disordered and perhaps seemingly disorganized, uncomfortable.

He looked at the oaken desk with its many drawers and despaired of finding what he was after. But, man does what he must. He sat himself down on the desk chair and decided where to begin.

The surface was clear and uncluttered. Probably Annette's doing. Like a roulette player throwing wildly, Columbo dropped his hand on the middle drawer on the left-hand side and pulled. He lost the bet. There was nothing here but years' worth of canceled checks, income tax returns, check-stubs and receipts.

Better luck next time.

Columbo pulled open the long thin center drawer and discovered a full collection of pencils, pens, markers, rulers, colored pencils and paper clips.

He shook his head negatively. He was so sure that he would find what he was after here.

He pulled the drawer out somewhat further. There in the very back filing the space between the pencils and the back wall of the drawer was a very slender stationery box. Orange letters marked it 'PRIVATE. A. BORCHARDT'. Columbo pulled it out and opening it found a sheaf of yellow papers from a legal pad. He hoped this would be what he wanted.

The top group (about ten sheets clipped together) looked like poetry. Not what the detective expected. The next item (three sheets, handwritten, paper-clipped) made up a letter. Undated it began 'Dear Henry . . .' It was addressed to Henry Thorne,

Chairman of the Board of Thorne Insurance Co. and President of the Board of Trustees.

When Columbo finished reading the letter, messily written, crossed out phrases and several drafts which were in the box behind it, he thought he had found that piece of the puzzle which he had been looking for.

The letter was a damning indictment of President Torrance and the whole administrative structure of Meredith College. Had this letter ever been typed out and mailed? If so it would provide reason enough for the President of the University to murder his Dean.

Thorne Insurance was headquartered in a thirty-three story building shaped like a large tombstone in downtown Los Angeles. Henry Thorne's office was on the thirty-third floor; in fact it was the thirty-third floor, the entire length and sweep of it, which the Chairman used as a penthouse office, private apartment and personal gymnasium. Columbo was shown into the gymnasium where Thorne, whom the detective recognized from the funeral, was standing on his hands on an exercise horse. 'Be right with you, Lieutenant.'

He stood another moment. Columbo looked around the room: it was a fully equipped gym, with a difference. It was carpeted and three telephones with external speakers were spotted strategically around so that Thorne could take a call from anywhere in the room including the trapeze and high bar.

Thorne flipped to his feet. 'Throw me that towel, would you?'

Columbo looked around himself and found a towel draped on a stand. 'This here?'

'Right.' He caught the towel and began wiping himself down. 'What can I do for you?'

'You're President of the Board of Trustees of Meredith College?'

'I suppose you're interested in Arnold Borchardt's murder?'

'Yes, sir. That's why I'm here.'

'Clearly. Follow me, Lieutenant.' Thorne led Columbo into a small dining room, also equipped with telephone. He pushed a button and invited Columbo to take a seat opposite him at the table.

A Mexican valet entered the room with a plate of cottage cheese, melba toast and a glass of ice tea. 'Anything for you?' Thorne asked. 'No thank you,' Columbo answered. 'I just want to go over a few things.'

'Don't mind if I eat, do you? After a workout you've got to eat something and if it's good lean food you keep good and lean and I believe a good lean body is the key to a good lean mind.'

Columbo nodded.

'Don't underestimate mind, Columbo. Mind is the great key to power. Money isn't worth a damn if you don't have the mind. What do you want to know.'

'I wonder if you'd take a look at this, sir.' Columbo handed Thorne the handwritten letter. 'And tell me if you ever received a formal copy?'

Thorne took the yellow sheets and read them over as he cracked melba toast in his mouth. 'No, he never sent that, Columbo. It's pretty strong stuff. I'd remember that.'

'Yes, sir. I'd think you would.'

'They are both capable men. Torrance and Borchardt. I've known Frank Torrance a very long time, Columbo. Twenty . . . twenty-five years. I don't put it past him to block Borchardt in all his attempts at bettering himself; the man was a real threat to Frank. But Frank wouldn't murder. *If* he even considered it, and I don't say he would, Frank is too fastidious to get involved with anything quite so messy as murder.' He took a swig of tea. 'And since Arnold never sent me that letter, Frank had no motive. And—' he paused to think – 'He wouldn't have a motive if the letter had been sent for the simple reason that we knew there was tension between the men, but we considered it a good creative tension.' He smiled at human folly. 'Those two, in their own ways are excellent for Meredith.'

'Well, sir. I think there was something else.'

'Something else?'

'Dean Borchardt seems a pretty loyal guy who wouldn't come running to the trustees unless it was his last play. He must have been thinking about it for a while or he wouldn't have written this, right?'

'He could've written it just to let off steam—'

'But he didn't send it. Why?'

Thorne nodded, finishing the last of his cottage cheese.

'Because . . . because there's something else. He found something out and that something was pretty damaging or he would have sent the letter. In other words,' Columbo was thinking aloud now, 'Borchardt had something pretty powerful against Torrance. Something strong enough to bust him loose *without* running to the trustees.'

'And when he used it, Frank killed Arnold.' Thorne stood up. 'Ridiculous. First of all, to suspect Frank Torrance of any violence is like suspecting Michelangelo . . . you know who Michelangelo was, Lieutenant?'

'Italian?'

'Right . . . of suspecting Michelangelo of destroying his own statues. Frank is an aesthetic, controlled, very rational man. That was our problem when we found Arnold Borchardt. Let me tell you what happened Lieutenant, and then maybe you'll understand:

'Nineteen sixty-eight was a tumultuous year. That was when we had all the revolutions on campuses around the country; all hell broke loose and Meredith was hardly exempt.

'Torrance is a very capable administrator but he has an aristocratic streak which I'm sure you've noticed? He handled the first protests capably if not with inspiration. Students picketed Meredith Hall and he issued nicely written – if not greatly relevant – statements. Then, November 21, a group of radical revolutionaries stormed Meredith Hall for a confrontation. Frank stood his ground, they stood theirs and the upshot was the occupation of Meredith and a head-on confrontation with its President. He was powerless, left the hall to the students and called in the police.

'Bad mistake. I bear some of the responsibility for that move. We talked it over at some length. But you know, Lieutenant, we trustees are shielded by a degree of anonymity, which provides us protection from visible scorn. Anyhow, the truth of the matter is that the police *did* come in, they used tear gas and made a godawful mess of things.

And worse yet, our problems weren't solved. They worsened. The radicals could now enlist the whole student body to their cause of a free-er, better, more amorphous education. Fat minds instead of lean if you ask me. Eight hundred or so of the student body took up residence outside Meredith Hall. They lived there. They sat around the building in a massive circle allowing no one in or out. They ate and slept and endured what little rain there was – I sometimes think this particular form of demonstration would not have happened if we weren't in California. Anyhow, we were desperate. Frank was obviously discredited by the use of police, and we needed someone else.

'Arnold Borchardt was in the English Department. He was one of the most popular teachers we've ever had. Something about his lectures drew students like bears to honey. His subject was obscure, really, very academic. Elizabethan and Jacobean literature. He did one course on Spenser's *The Faerie Queen* which did very well; but his Jacobean Theatre course was a sell-out. It wasn't the bloody melodramatic material, though that was part of it, but he had a gift for making it all sound so appropriate to today that you wouldn't believe!

'Anyhow, this man could reach students. So after much back and forth I called him down here – we didn't want any visible trustee meetings on campus – and asked him if he could break the siege.

'He was very reluctant, Columbo. He liked teaching and didn't like the idea of getting too mixed up in politics. But it was an emergency situation and he agreed to do what he could.

'Well, sir. I wish you could have seen that man in action. It was amazing. He stood up in front of those kids and started out with what sounded like a lecture in front of a black board. About right and wrong and self-respect and the real nature of revolution. And then he took off on that theme: revolution and training one's mind and body . . . I don't know how he did it, Columbo . . . it's still a mystery to me, but he had those wild kids eating out of his hand. The siege dispersed by midnight that same night and we agreed to the students' demand that Borchardt be made Dean of Students.

'Frank was jealous and tried to be gracious. But hell, he'd been humiliated. No question. On the other hand, he'd found a hell of a partner. The tension, we thought, might be workable, but I never imagined he would block Arnold from moving up in the academic world. Every letter I've written for the man has been favorable.' Thorne paused and looked at the yellow sheets he still held in his hand. 'But I've got to believe what he wrote here. Obviously Frank got wind of each application . . . he would. He would be asked for a reference no matter who Arnold recommended, and he probably sabotaged them in the most gracious and beautifully written put-downs.

'But that's hardly a motive for murder. Except possibly from Arnold's point of view. Hell, he had more cause to murder Frank than Frank did to murder him.'

'So it must have been something else,' said Columbo.

'I think you're making a terrible assumption there, Lieutenant. You're trying to find a motive to suit your theory of one man.'

'That's an honest criticism, Mr Thorne. It's about all I have to go on.'

'Well, don't go on this letter.'

'It started me thinking.'

'I think the murderer was someone off the street, myself. Or one of those kids who might have formed a grudge in the crowd way back in 1968 and finally, when everyone had forgotten, came and did the poor guy in.'

'It was two people, sir.'

'You're sure?'

'Pretty much.'

'That's your job Lieutenant. In any case, Arnold never sent this letter, which shows what a good friend he was to Frank Torrance.'

Columbo thanked Thorne for his time and left.

Driving back to Meredith he began thinking about the make-up stain on Torrance's cheek. It was too pink . . . too pink . . . Torrance had been on almost probationary ground (he figured) for the last five years. If there was one more thing against him . . . it could finish his career . . . there were only a couple of things that could really trump a college president: a drinking problem, cruelty or a woman – not just *any* woman either, but a student. Maybe Torrance *had* broken the unwritten rule . . . pink was a woman's skin color under the stage lights. Columbo figured he'd work that angle a bit.

CHAPTER 14

Vhile Columbo was driving the freeway from down-
own Los Angeles to Meredith, Torrance was letting
imself into Linda Kitteredge's house with his own key.
)pening the door was somewhat complicated by an
rmload of flowers and a fifth of Piper-Heidsick cham-
agne. He was happy to hear the shower running when
e entered the living-room. Linda was home and he
ould surprise her.

He found a vase in the kitchen and set the flowers out
n a low coffee table; he artfully arranged two glasses
nd the bottle of champagne near the flowers.

He went through the bedroom to the bathroom and
alled in a hello. Linda responded with a startled
What the hell are you doing here?'

'Don't ask. Bee to honey!'

'Oh, for God's sake!' The shower was suddenly
urned off and Linda appeared dripping wet, her long
londe hair dripping down her back. 'Hand me the
owel.'

As she dried herself she ranted. 'For an intelligent
nan you're not too bright. Do you have any idea of the
isk you're taking . . . ?' She went on matching her
ndignation to the violent motion of the towel as she
lried herself. Then, slipping into a bath-robe she
ooked over her shoulder at Torrance and said: 'You're
oing to have us both in the gas chamber. You know
hat?'

'I came a round-about way. No one saw me. No one will see me.'

Linda sat down at a dressing table in front of a large mirror. She began combing out her hair. Torrance came up behind her and put his hands on her shoulders. 'I thought the budding actress might enjoy a little celebration before her opening.'

'You're just horny.' But Linda smiled. 'It's stupid, Frank. It's only a stupid college production and if anybody saw you now . . .'

'Or any time.'

'But now especially, they'd put two and two together and it would come out a terrible zero for both of us.'

Torrance sat on the bed. 'I decided to take this opening seriously. Part of the problem here was that I didn't take student affairs seriously.'

'Student affairs!' she snorted.

He smiled. 'Not quite what I meant.'

'Frank! your timing is dismal. Not only isn't this a very important "student affair" . . . the play I mean . . . *but*, you know: we killed him. And if that little detective ever gets a whiff of our relationship, we're skunked.'

'I love watching you comb your hair.'

'Are you being wilfully stupid?' She turned away from the mirror and fixed a killing look on him.

'You're in quite a mood.'

'Damn it, Frank! You can't be that dumb!'

'You listen to me, Linda.' He stood up. 'I know damn well what I'm doing. I came to be nice and show you that in spite of everything you've gotten us into, I'm still with you.'

'Oh, Big! Big! *I've* gotten us into this.'

'It was your idea to kill Arnold Borchardt.' He said this very quietly. 'And let's not forget it.'

'You weren't shy about it big shot!'

'Therefore: if affection isn't enough to hold us, then that little blood tie is.'

'I told you what I think of affection.' She turned back to the mirror and began brushing her hair vigorously with firm violent strokes.

'I've got something else to tell you.'

'Tell me!'

'Later.' Torrance went into the living room and sat down. He stared at the roses. He counted them to be sure there was an even two dozen. He thought of counting the petals and thorns. Linda stayed in her room. He hoped she was combing her hair. It would have to look particularly perfect tonight; though at her age she always looked perfect. He hated her and he loved her. He hated her youth and he found it exciting. He felt he was getting old and he wished he hadn't chosen to play this foolish game of out-waiting and trying to out-wit her.

Linda wasn't combing her hair. She was sitting dully staring at herself in the mirror. Frank had never brought her to tears. Very few people ever had. And she'd be damned if she let him get away with it now. She wasn't going to let him best her. Never. Never. She picked up the brush and pulled it listlessly through her hair. But it was no good . . . she put it down and stood up. Damn!

When she came out of the bedroom door she saw the roses and the champagne and couldn't help smiling. 'You're like a teenager,' she said, smiling.

'I try to keep young as best I can.'

Linda fell into his lap. He kissed her gently. She ran her hand through his hair. He slid his right hand into her robe and felt her soft silken skin. Every time he touched her the excitement was overwhelming. But she didn't want to be mussed up, not now. She had too little time and the performance ahead.

'I was thinking,' he said, 'during intersession. Come to Europe with me a couple of weeks.'

'What about your wife?' Linda sat up and disengaged his hand.

'I told her I had a conference and she should meet me when it's over. But what I really want is two weeks with you . . .'

'What'll I tell my parents?'

'We'll think of something.'

She stood up and walked to the flowers. 'You're trying to get rid of me aren't you?'

'I didn't say that.'

'I'm not stupid. It's two weeks in Europe and then kiss-off, goodbye.'

'I wasn't thinking—'

She spun around angrily: 'You weren't thinking, period! You don't think! What happened the day before yesterday was just that: unthinking! You don't know yourself, Frank. Not at all!'

'I don't think that was my motive . . .' He spoke in carefully measured tones. 'But you could be right, Linda. I might have been looking for a graceful way out of this relationship.'

'You talk like a goddamned book sometimes.'

'I hadn't *really* considered it seriously that way. But . . . when you said it . . . I'll acknowledge. You might be right.'

'Graceful way out . . . !' She picked up the champagne bottle and cradled it in her hands. 'Piper-Heidsick. Only the best.'

'I had good motives this afternoon.'

'Right.' She replaced the bottle next to the roses. 'You're really something, Mr President!'

'You forget a few things, Linda. You forget that you told me yourself you would walk out of this affair whenever you chose. You have never made me any promises.'

'That holds. I'm not going to be tied down to anyone.'

'You forget that we are locked into a death-grip with each other because of this Borchardt thing and damn it all, we're better off apart. That's the practicality.'

'Then why Europe? Why are you here now? Why don't you just walk out and forget it.'

Weakly, his face crumpling into a pudding of self pity, the President of Meredith College, who had served on many government commissions; whose ambitions had once included high government appointment; who had known presidents, muttered: 'I can't. I just can't.'

Linda turned and seeing that expression began to laugh . . . to laugh long, and loud and triumphantly. 'Oh, you poor fool! You poor goddamned stupid fool!' she said finally. 'We never could have a future! Never! Never!' And her laughter consumed her.

Torrance, stung, stood up suddenly and crossed the room. He grabbed her left arm with his left hand slapped her across the face. 'Bitch!'

'Murderous bitch,' she spat back at him! 'Murderous bloody awful bitch!' She broke away from him. 'You know, I admired you. A little bit. Until last night. To hell with Europe. Get out.'

'It's pleasant to see you can get upset about something.' Torrance walked out of the house, then, for the first time since their relationship began, he forgot to look to see if anyone was coming along who might recognize him. Fortunately, nobody was and he walked back to his office unseen.

An unhappy walk. Torrance had to admit to himself that he loved the girl; or at least loved something in her besides her youth and beauty. They were a good pair, a fine match. Yet, he also knew that she would never marry him and that he would never give up Hilda. Hilda had been the wife for his early years; a woman from a fine New York family with wealth and social connections to match his. They were, in their first years, the perfect academic-foundation couple. Well-connected, at ease in the world which cut across Wall Street and Fifth Avenue. This was the world of the Eastern Establishment with its web weaving through the major newspapers, foundations, government and educational institutions from Harvard to Georgetown University in Washington D.C. Hilda had suited him wonderfully in those years and her wit and quickness of mind had been an asset as valuable as her family connections and dignified handsome beauty.

But after the move to California and the Presidency of Meredith, they had both changed. Torrance had somehow removed himself from the pulses of life and Linda suited this removal perfectly. She combined an aloof and cynical nature with a kind of objective sensuality which matched his moods. But she was too young and his ways were set and there would have come an end to their affair sooner or later; better it be now before they did themselves more harm.

Torrance was not pleased to see Columbo waiting for him when he entered his office. Even less pleased when Columbo asked him (again) whether he knew much more about a student named Linda Kitteredge.

'You asked me about that girl once, Columbo. Why again? I don't know anything about her.'

'Well, sir. She might be mixed up in this thing. I talked to this fellow Peter Arminski who was the only other person to see Mr Borchardt before he died and I'm pretty sure he's got nothing to do with it. And I don't feel so sure about this Kitteredge girl.'

'We've thousands of students, Columbo.'

'Not too many were in the theatre the night of the murder.'

Torrance walked to the office door and asked Miss Purdom to bring Linda Kitteredge's file to him. 'She's the one playing the lead tonight?'

'I think so, sir. Yes.'

'Why should she want to kill her director? Especially just before opening night?'

'Well, sir, I don't know. But of course if my theory is correct, she wasn't acting alone.'

'Maybe it was a team of assassins, Lieutenant!'

Miss Purdom entered with the file. Torrance opened it. 'Let's see what we've got here. Ah, yes. Here Lieutenant . . .' Torrance felt very nervous, tense. He had really been frightened once yesterday morning.

Columbo looked over the entries. Born May 17, 1953, Orlando, Florida. Living in Houston, Texas when she applied to Meredith. A good interview report from the admissions director, test scores . . . very good. Academic record . . . a straight 'A' student. 'Bright girl,' Columbo muttered.

'Let's see.' Torrance reached for the file again. He felt, inexplicably, that he was in some kind of contest. He pretended to look down the rows of grades. 'Yes. Looks like pre-med to me.'

Columbo asked for the file again. 'Something funny.'

He leafed through. 'Here.' He showed Torrance. 'That's not a dormitory is it?'

'The address. No. She lives off campus. Many of our students do these days, Columbo.'

'Can't blame them I guess.'

'Hardly.'

'Must be inconvenient if you're pre-med and have all those labs. and stuff.'

'That's for the student to work out. These are adult human beings, Lieutenant. The days when a university administration played surrogate parent is over.'

Columbo shook his head. 'Well, I guess there's nothing here. Thanks.' He handed the file back to Torrance and started for the door. 'Oh, yeah. I was thinking, just this one question. When you were at the theater last night, you talked to Dean Borchardt?'

'A moment. Yes.'

'You know he was having a lot of trouble finding a new job?'

'I'm sorry to hear that, Columbo.'

Columbo scratched his head. 'Funny, because everybody I talk to except you says he was something very special in this business.'

'What are you trying to say, Lieutenant?'

'Everybody who he applied to . . . they'd always end up asking you about him, wouldn't they?'

'We worked together. Certainly. I was his immediate superior.'

'You didn't like him too much.'

'I didn't sabotage him, Lieutenant.'

'I was thinking that if you didn't like him you'd want to get rid of him.'

'Lieutenant!' Torrance was angry. 'I didn't kill him.

And I don't like subtle innuendo. Say right out what you have to say but for God's sake stop trying to get under my skin. Ask me point blank, if that's what you're thinking.'

'I'm sorry. I'm really . . . I owe you an apology. No. No. I was thinking that you'd want him out of the University if you didn't like him and so give him good references.'

'Well, in all honesty, Lieutenant. I didn't think he was fit to run a major institution.'

'And you told this to people?'

'Yes. I owed it to the institutions to tell them my thoughts.'

'Did Mr Borchardt know this?'

'He suspected it, surely. But those are the breaks of the game.'

'Yeah. Well, thanks.' Again Columbo headed for the door.

'What are you getting at, Lieutenant?'

Columbo turned. 'Just trying to figure this out. There was a lot of animosity between you?'

'Arnold had more cause to kill me than I had to kill him.'

'Yeah. But it didn't work out that way.'

'Lieutenant: I'm very busy. With him gone, I've got a double load for a while. Will you excuse me?'

'Sure. Sure. See you tonight.' Columbo was out the door.

Torrance was worried. 'Tonight?' he asked himself and remembered the play opening. Damn . . . he wished the investigation were over. Columbo was like a hunting dog, digging, digging. There was no way to link Torrance with the killing . . . but if there were, some small detail overlooked, Columbo would find it. 'I've been very stupid,' Torrance thought to himself. 'I can't control events any more. I can only wait!'

His mood was hardly improved when he returned home that evening and Hilda asked him if he'd ever heard of a student named Linda Kitteredge. 'Why the hell do you want to know that?' he exploded. Hilda explained about her conversation with Columbo in the parking lot after the memorial service.

Torrance felt that it had been a very long day, with, unfortunately more to come.

CHAPTER 15

Meredith Playhouse was bathed in light. Crowds gathered outside on its spacious lawns waiting for the last moment of quiet blue evening to fade before going inside for the first performance of *The White Devil*. Cars drove in a steady stream into the parking lot. The atmosphere would have been that of a formal professional opening if so many of the audience weren't dressed in casual California clothes.

Columbo pulled his battered Mercedes, chugging noticeably, to a stop on the street opposite the theater. Approaching the playhouse, he was struck by the large number of beards in evidence. Students and faculty were impressively hirsute and could only be told apart by their dress, the faculty tending toward slightly more formal attire.

President Torrance stood in sharp contrast to the others by virtue of his dark pin-striped suit. He would never break certain East Coast habits. He stood with Hilda and Dean Markham and his wife, a small very, very round woman, whom one could easily picture pitching into a full plate of spaghetti and meat sauce and then perhaps another and another after that.

Markham hailed Columbo enthusiastically. 'Monday night was your night to shine, Columbo; tonight the Meredith Masquers! Such are the riches of life!' Markham was hearty and clapped Columbo on the back.

'Well, sir. I'm sure it'll be interesting.'

'For you, Lieutenant, grist for the mill. This play is murder and betrayal piled upon murder and betrayal in an absolutely sinful manner. By God! If I were a detective I'd enjoy the swirling plots and counterplots. What about you, Frank?'

'I'd venture our detective friend has a real life problem complicated enough for him.'

'Ah, the Borchardt case. Is that true, Columbo?'

'Actually, I expect to get it settled tonight.'

'While you watch the play. Very cool, Columbo. Very cool indeed. Very Sherlock Holmes, if I may say so.' Markham invited Columbo to join his party, but the detective begged off, saying he'd rather stand in the back of the theatre. Then he excused himself, but, turning suddenly, he caught Torrance looking at him. 'Excuse me, sir,' he asked the startled President, 'but I'll be looking for you later, so I hope you'll stay until I've talked to you after the play.'

'A bust coming, Columbo?' Markham prided himself on being up-to-date in his language.

'Mr Torrance should be on hand if the murderer is apprehended.'

'Responsibilities, Frank. I'm happy to be a lowly dean.'

Torrance wondered what the hell was going on.

Backstage a kind of quiet hysteria reigned. The chaos from the night before had been replaced by a calm desperation. Everyone was going through the motions of preparing for a performance but with none of the vigor, energy or enthusiasm that usually attends these events. Actors, stage-hands, electricians, dressers, stage-managers were functioning like automata. They knew their roles and performed them.

Columbo wandered through this taut atmosphere

unnoticed. He had the feeling that he'd become so familiar to them all in the last twenty-four hours that he was considered a mere prop like the chairs, coffins and swords.

Familiar, himself, with the backstage layout of the theater, Columbo made his way over coiled cables, in and out of painted flats, past hanging ropes, to the corridor which led to the women's dressing room. Outside the door he asked a girl, who was doing ballet exercises in a leotard and skirt, to send Linda out to him.

Even Columbo, who had seen much in his life, gasped a little when he saw Linda made up for her first performance. Her hair had been enhanced by a high sculptured hair-piece intertwined with jewels (fake). Her ice-blue gown complemented her pink skin and caught the diamond hardness of her eyes. Her naturally clear skin was made translucent by make-up – the color Columbo remembered from Torrance's cheek. She was, indeed, an impressive beauty.

'Gee, I'm sorry to bother you at a moment like this, but I was going over a few things in my mind and was wondering . . .'

'Be quick, Lieutenant.' She was taut and very nervous. Jumpy.

'This won't take a minute. I was wondering if in all the times rehearsing the play and discussing problems with Mr Borchardt if . . . did he ever say anything to you about his problems with Mr Torrance?'

'Oh, really, Columbo! You're too much!'

'Well, I was thinking you let your hair down with people like this in a situation like rehearsals. Everybody's working together . . . maybe he let something slip and you'd remember.'

'Couldn't this wait until after the performance?'

'I've heard things about students and faculty . . .'

'What kind of things!' Linda snapped before she was aware of what she was saying or her attitude.

'The kind of thing you were telling me didn't happen very much – between faculty and students. Affairs? They happen—'

Linda laughed coldly. 'This isn't a convent, Lieutenant. Sure they happen. But they're not encouraged.'

'And I was wondering if Mr Borchardt ever let anything out about Mr Torrance.'

'Like they were having an affair? Please!'

'In confidence. No joking, Miss Kitteredge. They didn't like each other too much did they?'

The stage manager hustled through yelling 'Five minutes! Five minutes!'

'I can't talk to you now, Lieutenant.'

'I've got reason to believe that Mr Torrance was somehow sabotaging Mr Borchardt's attempts to get work somewhere else. Well, Mr Borchardt was going to complain to the trustees, but he found out something about Mr Torrance that he could use to blackmail him with. It's just a theory of course, but I was wondering if there was anything in all the times you were alone with Mr Borchardt that he let slip what he knew or even a hint?'

'No!' Linda seemed strangely keyed up and frantic. 'I'm sure I can take your word on that.'

'I can't concentrate on what you're saying. The curtain's going up any minute.' Just then a voice came over the intercom system: 'Places! Places!' Columbo could feel the electricity shoot through the air. 'Yeah! Good luck!' he said.

The last of the audience were filing into their seats

when Columbo returned to the auditorium. He managed to catch Torrance as he was taking his seat. 'If I could just say a word, sir.'

Torrance helped Hilda out of her coat and then came out into the aisle with Columbo. 'What is it now, Lieutenant? The curtain's about to go up.'

A trumpet fanfare played through the loudspeakers.

'I hear that sir.' The lights began their slow dim into the magical and promising darkness preceding the curtain's rise. 'I just wondered if Mr Borchardt . . . well, sir, might be having an affair with Miss Kitteredge—'

'You're out of your mind, Columbo!' Torrance was whispering now, in high heat.

The trumpet voluntary repeated.

'It's not impossible, sir.'

'Nothing's impossible. But he'd be in worse trouble than she.' Drums were added to the trumpets. 'It's frowned on. It's unethical for a teacher to sleep with a student.'

'I guess you're right. But I've got the impression that's what was going on.'

People began hushing the two of them and the curtain started its slow ascent on the scene, a street in Rome.

'I'll talk to you later, sir.' Columbo hurried up the aisle to stand in the back. Torrance took his seat. Columbo found a place to stand in the rear to one side of the auditorium where he could keep an eye on Torrance as he watched the play.

A street in Rome . . . conspirators whispering urgently in the shadows. Then a shift, the street is gone and in its place a hanging carpet, some tables, chairs, a mirror:

the furnishings of an Italian Renaissance Court. Enter Brachiano, several others and Vittoria Corombona (Linda Kitteredge). The two touch hands, look at one another, circle and draw closer. Speak. She tells him of her dream which suggested that her husband and Brachiano's wife must die. They arrange their assignation. The scene ends with Flamineo, Vittoria's evil brother sneaking off after summing up the treacherous action:

We are engaged to mischief, and must on:
As rivers to find out the ocean . . .
the way ascends not straight, but imitates
the subtle foldings of a winter snake . . .

The scene shifts again: another palace suggested by a simple change in the backdrop and a new arrangement of furniture. Friends of Brachiano's wife, having heard of Brachiano's affair with Vittoria warn him:

When you awake from this lascivious dream,
Repentence will follow, like the sting
placed in the adder's tail.

Hearing these words, Torrance shifted nervously in his seat. The word 'repentance' echoed in his mind. He made a mental note to ask Linda whether she believed in it . . . and then he heard . . .

lust carries her sharp whip
At her own girdle . . .

and fancied that Hilda looked at him accusingly. But when he turned to his left she sat absorbed in the interplay between the three young male actors. Looking right he noticed Columbo in the shadows. Was the detective watching him? *Lust* – strange sound, harsh driving emotion . . . was that all he felt for Linda? Had he been seduced by lust not love? Was he just another old fool falling for a lithsome young body? No. No. No. He'd always guarded himself against just that. But the doubt . . . the murder . . . ?

The repercussions of the affair between Brachiano and Vittoria continued to thunder across the stage. A harsh and terrible scene between Brachiano and his wife Isabella where he tells her he can never be a real husband to her again. Her despair, gently portrayed by a blonde actress, eighteen years old. Torrance was startled by the effect the youthful actress had on the part. Here was no sophisticated worldly older woman suffering rejection at the hands of a tough-minded cynical man. It was a young girl, vulnerable, who could only be in the first flush of marriage and love, cast off for someone colder and harsher. You had to feel that Brachiano was a villain, an insensitive selfish lubricious brute ignoring a clear mountain stream in order to drink brackish and polluted waters. Torrance felt he too was a brute. Hilda was a fine intelligent woman . . . and Linda . . . Linda . . .

A murder plot followed, Brachiano plotting to kill his wife and Vittoria's husband in conjunction with an unscrupulous doctor. With all the pieces in place, murder, discovery and revenge must follow from the adulterous lust of these two people.

In a scene which brought shock, surprise and pleasure to Columbo, whose experience of theater was minimal, and spontaneous wild applause from the audience, the murders were played out, but hardly as expected: a magician came to Brachiano and called up the scenes of the murders to music while the dancers illustrated the bloody deaths in stylized pantomimic movement.

First: two plotters enter and draw back a curtain, unveiling Brachiano's picture. They put on protective glasses which cover eyes and nose and burn certain perfumes in front of the portrait and smear the lips with an invisible poison. They exit laughing. Isabella, Brachiano's wife enters in her nightgown on her way to bed. She kneels down to her prayers after which she draws the curtain to the picture and kisses it three times. She faints, dies. Lodovico and Giovanni enter and carry off her corpse.

The lights die. The music fades on the scene and Brachiano exclaims: 'Excellent! Then she's dead!' The magician nods 'yes' and snaps his fingers.

Torrance felt a chill. Hilda noticed the shudder and looked at him; then she took his hand to comfort him. 'Nerves,' he muttered to himself.

Columbo didn't miss a beat of the little scene in the audience.

Onstage again: the conjurer called up a second scene for Brachiano to witness; the lights shifted again; other-worldly, supernatural music came up: Flamineo, Marcello and Vittoria's husband, Camillo enter. The room itself is set up as a Renaissance Italian gymnasium, with tumbling mats and vaulting horses. Camillo does a couple of exercise turns on the horse, when suddenly he is seized from behind by Flamineo, the others hold him and snap-bang, his neck is broken. He is arranged under the horse in a position suggesting an accidental fall. Brachiano comments: 'Twas quaintly done.'

The murders described now, the magician spoke: 'Both flowers and weeds spring when the sun is warm And great men do great good or else great harm.'

Torrance felt himself suffocating in the dark auditorium. The crumpled body of the dead Camillo under the horse flashed an image of the unconscious Borchardt through his mind. Crumpled lying under the saw horses under the coffin. He seemed to play over and over again, like the endless loop of a movie spliced to itself, his hand holding the pipe coming down behind the dean's ear . . . and again . . . his hand slowly coming down behind the dean's ear . . . when beyond the broken skin and the snapping neck Torrance saw for the first time what he had refused to see before: Linda's expression. Wide-eyed startled delight . . . yes *delight* . . . her eyes luminous in the backstage shadows. In slow motion his memory played Borchardt's fall and he could not believe . . . did not . . . would not believe . . . but her eyes, the attitude of her body, the sudden spreading of her hands and fingers all spoke an eagerness to pounce, like a vampire . . . something frightening and supernatural. He tried to rub these ideas away, to blank the images from his consciousness, but he could not . . . they would not go. He felt nausea welling up and feared movement, feared Columbo would notice his agitation and link it with the murder on stage and then *know*! He forced his organs to behave, but could not stop the flash of sweat that broke in a film across his body. Hilda leaned over. 'Are you sick?'
'A little, but it's alright. Alright!'

From the shadows, Columbo noted the agitation.

When Torrance regained his composure and focused again on the stage he saw Linda/Vittoria. She stood now in a courtroom: again a rearrangement of furniture and change of lights and backcloths, Vittoria on trial, accused of the murder of her husband.

Torrance watched her accused:

She's like the guilty counterfeited coin
Which whosoe'er first stamps it, brings trouble to
all that receive it.
Next the devil adultery, enters the devil murder . . .

But the accusations are vague, for Vittoria could not have broken her husband's neck herself, yet her accusers know that through her affair with Brachiano, the two of them are responsible for the murders.

My Lord, there's great suspicion of the murder,
But no sound proof who did it. For my part I do not
think
She hath a soul so black
To act a deed so bloody:

Yet how fierce and fiery her defense. So fierce, impressive and strong, in fact, that Linda made the chandeliers ring above the audience's head, her words were fire streaming from her mouth; her eyes flashed knives of hate and defiance.

You are deceived!
For know, that all your strict combine'd heads,
Which strike against this mine of diamonds,
Shall prove glassen hammers – they shall break.
These are but feigned shadows of my evils:
Terrify babes, my lord, with painted devils;
I am past such needless palsy. For your names
of whore and murderess, they proceed from you,
As if a man should spit against the wind;
The filth return's in's face . . .

So harsh, true, venomous and powerful was Linda's speech that the audience fairly gasped at the end of it.

Condemn you me for that the duke did love me!
So may you blame some fair and crystal river

For that some melancholic distracted man
Hath drowned himself in it!
Sum up my faults, I pray, and you shall find,
That beauty, and gay clothes, a merry heart,
And a good stomach to a feast are all,
All the poor crimes that you can charge me with.

Beautiful proud woman. 'If the devil did ever take good shape, behold this picture,' says one of her accusers referring to Vittoria.

At that moment, as surely as though he had seen it all happen, Columbo, alone in the shadows, watching Torrance and Linda . . . the one in the dark, the other ablaze in stage lights, knew what had happened and why Borchardt had been killed.

Before the curtain fell on intermission, Vittoria was sentenced to spend the rest of her years in a 'house of penitent whores' a kind of holy place for the rehabilitation of fallen women.

And Vittoria responded:

O woman's poor revenge.
Which dwells but in the tongue! I will not weep;
No, I do scorn to call up one poor tear
To fawn on your injustice; bear me hence
Unto this house . . . !

The lobby buzzed with praise for what the young actors and Borchardt (rest him) had accomplished with this difficult obscure play. Circulating among the excited people, Columbo heard nothing but formidable praise for Linda's performance; so full of conviction and certainty. He decided there was nothing people liked more than a beautiful villainess.

*

'Well, Lieutenant Columbo,' pale, his voice not quite so firm as usual, Torrance hailed the detective, 'What do you think of our thespians?'

Columbo looked blank.

'Actors!'

'That Kitteredge girl she's quite something!'

'They're a fine group. Coming in from outside, could you solve a murder where a woman kissed a portrait and was poisoned.'

'We might not get the portrait part. But the poison's in the blood. Simple autopsy.'

'Modern technology! It takes the poetry out of murder, doesn't it, Lieutenant?'

'You know, Mr Torrance, there's no poetry in murder. Killing's just a plain ugly and bloody business. I've handled enough cases that I've seen some of these, what people call, crimes of passion. Like this one here on stage. Murder for love . . . ?' He seemed thoughtful a moment, marshalling his words. Torrance wondered what he was getting at. Columbo continued, deliberately, 'But it's ugly, see. Killing. And the ugliness and the shock of it to the murderer kind of soaks in. Sometimes it goes fast and sometimes it goes slow. But it soaks in and then the murderer traps himself very often. All I have to do is sit back and wait for that little thing to happen. I don't know what it is, but when it happens I recognize it and well . . . that's it then.'

'Are you at that stage with the Borchardt case, Lieutenant?'

The buzz of lobby conversation camouflaged the intensity of the words stalking back and forth between Columbo and Torrance.

'I think so, sir.' Columbo spoke quietly, politely.

'And what I'm going to say is going to surprise you . . .' He looked over his shoulder left and right. No one overhearing. The bells announcing the Act Two curtain rang. 'I'm sure now that Miss Kitteredge has something to do with it!'

The audience began filing into the auditorium. Hilda Torrance who had been talking with a group nearby, took Torrance's hand. 'Come along dear. You look terrible.' To Columbo, she said, 'He hasn't been feeling well.'

'Nothing serious. I think you're on the wrong track there, Columbo.'

'Maybe . . . anyhow, thought you should know.'

The lobby had almost emptied and Torrance excused himself to return to his seat. On the way down the aisle, Hilda asked Torrance what Columbo was on the 'wrong track' about. 'The murder!' he answered brusquely. 'But he's all wrong. It doesn't make any sense.' Hilda wanted to know what didn't make any sense. 'Linda Kitteredge . . .' he muttered as he sank back into his seat. The lights were already dimming.

'The white devil?' Hilda was startled.

Act Two. Music. Trumpets, drums, the sweet liquid sound of a viola da gamba added to the instruments. The curtain rises. The scene was still a Renaissance mansion. The aggrieved relatives of the murdered wife and Vittoria's husband stood plotting their revenge on all those responsible.

Francisco de Medici was consulting a catalogue of known murderers looking for one to perform the vengeful tasks for him.

Linda stood in the wings, off-stage, her costume changed now for a simple gray gown, the mark of

Vittoria's captivity. She watched the actor playing Francisco reading the list, looking for someone to do his dirty work for him.

The scene ended. She watched the stage hands shift sets: all the sumptuous carpets and hangings were removed; the elaborately carved and inlaid furnishings carried away. Four flats painted to resemble unadorned stone walls descended from the flies. Two rude wooden benches and a plain trestle table were carried on and fixed into place. The lighting shifted to a mixture of blues and whites, rendering the set cold and formidably stark. As the scene progressed small side spots of red would be added to the lights, giving a luminous definition to the bloody deeds about to follow.

Flamineo was onstage intercepting a letter meant for Vittoria. Linda took a deep breath. She heard the lines leading to her cue.

FLAMINEO: As in this world there are degrees of evils.
So in this world there are degrees of devils.

Brachiano cursed Flamineo. (Pander!) . . . Flamineo, himself a murderer, rejoined. She heard him speak and listened for the word that would draw her inexorably back onto the stage . . . 'whirlpool' . . .

She entered. She thrilled, as always at the paradoxical privacy of the stage world: it was the convent, a wall of light separating her from the audience and adding a special atmosphere to the stage through its warmth. Beyond the wall of light, she felt the audience tauten with anticipation. It sent a thrill through her body. She spoke her first line – a cold response to Brachiano's accusation that she clandestinely received love letters from many men: 'Say, sir?' And it was cold and perfectly spoken, like an ice-cube spit into his face.

Those two words hooked into the audience's gills as surely as if they were so many fish.

The scene was again one of reply, self-defense . . . Vittoria, now called 'the devil in crystal' was set upon by Brachiano, her lover:

That hand, that cursed hand, which I have wearied with doting kisses.
My loose thoughts scatter like quicksilver: I was bewitched;
For all the world speaks ill of thee.

Hearing those words, Linda, inadvertently (it hadn't been rehearsed that way) smiled. The thought of Frank Torrance bewitched by her, passed through her mind. Now she was playing against him, not the boy-actor trying to play a man-lover. The shift in object gave her performance a startling, electric reality.

No matter: I'll live so now, I'll make that world recant,
And change her speeches . . .

And a moment later, sweeping around one of two benches, her head thrown back with scorn and haughtiness:

What have I gained by thee but infamy?
Thou hast stained the spotless honour of my house,
And frighted thence noble society:
. . . What do you call this house?
Is this your palace/did not the judge style it
A house of penitent whores? Who sent me to it?
. . . Go, Go, brag how many ladies you have undone like me.
Fare you well, sir; let me hear no more of you!
I'll not shed one tear more – I'll burst first!

She flung herself away from Brachiano crossing behind the table and standing looking out into the wings, her arms crossed, her back expressing all her anger, remembering how, this afternoon she'd refused to let Torrance bring her to tears and had driven him from her house!

But looking into the wings she was startled to see Columbo, standing there, calmly watching the action. She lost a beat, shuddered, causing Brachiano in his speech to repeat her name three times: Vittoria! Vittoria! *Vittoria!* instead of just the one time in the script.

He was penitent now, looking for forgiveness. With relief, she turned away, from Columbo's steady eyes.

When it came time for her exit, Linda left the stage into the wing opposite Columbo. The pace of action sped up now. Lodovico, the hired killer, ended the following scene in front of a church with the line: 'Now to the act of blood.'

Brachiano was ingeniously killed when he put on a poisoned helmet. The poison seeped through his skull into his brain driving him crazy. Vittoria attended his death and her exit afterwards, consumed with grief ('Oh me! This place is hell!') took her finally back to where Columbo was standing.

She stopped, shocked from the change of worlds, onstage to off. She took a deep breath. 'What are you doing back here, Lieutenant?'

'I'm very impressed,' he answered. 'That's some acting out there!'

'Thanks!'

'You going on again?'

'I still have to die.'

'I've never seen a play with so much dying and

killing. But then I haven't been to too many plays. My wife, she likes to go sometimes.'

'You know if you weren't a police officer you wouldn't be allowed back here during a performance.'

'I don't want to be in the way. Say, I thought you'd be interested in something . . .'

'Hurry up. I have to go on again.'

The scene changed quickly to a street and quickly again to another of the sumptuous settings with carpets, drapes, ornate furnishings: Vittoria's palace.

Anticipating her entrance, Linda licked her lips to brighten her lipstick.

'I think I've got a good line on who killed Mr Borchardt?'

'Who?'

'I think Mr Torrance's got something to do with it.'

The lights crashed up on the set, a mixture of blood-reds and violent violets. 'Jesus!' she muttered under her breath and sailed onto the stage.

She was definitely unnerved, but the edge gave her acting an even more erratic excitement than before. She had been good, now she was unstable in her language, her voice quavered, and it sent shivers through the audience.

Flamineo threatened her with pistols. She tricked him into letting her shoot him first and then she said she would shoot herself. *But* Flamineo was, in truth, tricking Vittoria. The shots she fired from his gun were blanks and he rose from his false death in a murderous fury. She screamed for help and the hired assassin, Lodovico, entered with his henchmen. Seeing that her time was up, Vittoria turned magnificent: the lines, coupled to the real fear trembling in her, gave Linda a power and stature that was breathtaking:

I shall welcome death
As princes do some great ambassadors;
I'll meet thy weapon halfway . . .
LODOVICO: Thou dost tremble.
Methinks fear should dissolve thee into air.

Inadvertently, Linda looked toward the wings. Columbo stood there, like a threatening angel. To the audience her odd turning away seemed as though she were trying to escape Lodovico's inevitable dagger thrust. Columbo turned away and walked out of her sight. She turned her head back toward the action, stark cold fear trembling in her voice:

O, thou art deceived. I am too true a woman:
Conceit can never kill me. I'll tell thee what,
I will not in my death shed one base tear;
Or if look pale, for want of blood, not fear

Lodovico cried 'Strike! Strike!' The dagger thrust into her belly, her breast. She cried 'Twas a manly blow,' and burst a small plastic container of stage blood against her breast. Another against her stomach. When Lodovico stepped away from in front of her the blood seemed to pour from the two spots:

'O!' she cried, 'my greatest sin lay in my blood.
Now my blood pays for it!'

Columbo walked up the far aisle of the auditorium. The audience sat riveted in darkness. His eyes searched out Torrance. He sat frozen, watching a spectre perform in front of him. The man had grown so pale he almost glowed white in the dark.

Vittoria/Linda spoke her next-to-last line before

dying: 'My soul like to a ship in a black storm, is driven. I know not whither.'

When she died a newer deeper stillness washed over the audience like a wave. It was only left for Flamineo, the last villain to be killed and for Giovanni, Brachiano's young son and now the heir to all the bloody miseries of the Renaissance court to speak the final lines before curtain:

Let guilty men remember, their black deeds
Do lean on crutches made of slender reeds.

The lights blacked out, there was a pause as seven hundred and thirty-three people in the audience took a deep breath and then the applause broke like a thunderclap. The lights went up on the large cast, bowing together in their ornate costume.

Linda, everyone noticed, applauding even wilder, was crying. Tears streamed down her face without stop, streaking her make-up, imparting a shine to her eyes that everyone mistook for triumph.

CHAPTER 16

A series of interconnected rehearsal rooms underneath the main theatre had been turned into a large reception room for guests following the performance. It was customary for friends, relatives, faculty and administration to gather and toast the first night of a student production. Tonight the crowd hummed with Linda's praises; many, who had been at Meredith for years, felt that they had never seen a performance to rival her Vittoria Corombona. She was, by common consensus, one of the most enormously gifted actresses to pass through the college. '. . . and she's a pre-med student!' gasped one gray-haired, large-busted faculty wife. 'Can you imagine? To just find the time, much less the talent for such a thing!'

The crowd was large and pressing. Torrance, feeling weak and sick, could not find enough open space or air. So, he tried to expand his consciousness a bit with scotch. Hilda tried to slow down his consumption of beverage, but he wouldn't listen to her. He kept looking nervously around the room.

'What's the matter with you, Frank?' Hilda asked. 'You've acted strange all evening. If you're sick I'll take you home.'

'I'm not sick. Merely deeply affected by the extraordinary performances.' And he looked around again.

'What *are* you looking for?'

'Not what – who? Lieutenant Columbo hinted before the play that he'd have some information bearing on the Borchardt case.' He took a long swig of liquor. 'Borchardt . . . dead duck, dead dean . . . have you noticed Hilda how bloody these revenge tragedies are . . . and how justice is . . . bloodily dished out at the end . . . murderers murdered . . . avengers avenged,' he muttered and drank.

The man he was looking for, Columbo, was in the hallway outside the reception room. He was talking to the law school Dean Markham. Then, seeing the stage manager Mary Jane Francis at the far end of the corridor near the dressing rooms, he excused himself from Markham to catch up with her.

Markham joined the party and found Torrance. 'Just been talking to our resident detective, Lieutenant Columbo. He says he's cracked the case and wants to meet you at your office at midnight. I hope he's right.'

'Why did he tell you and not me!'

'Don't get angry, Frank.'

'Frank has been acting peculiar all evening.' Hilda interjected. 'I really think he's coming down with something.'

'Bloody colic,' he burped.

'Frank, you're a disgrace tonight.' Hilda was really angry. 'I'm going to talk to Elsie Birch!' She stormed off through the crowd toward a tall red-haired lady across the room.

Markham tried to pick up the slack. 'That Kitteredge girl was impressive, Frank.'

'Impressive, beautiful girl. Damned if she didn't seem to be the real thing up there. Real, whore, murderess, duchess . . . inciting to murder . . . turning men around her little finger . . . victimizing victims . . .'

'You are in a mood aren't you?'

'Why the hell shouldn't I?'

'What's eating you?'

'Death . . . the grim reaper. I've had my goddamned fill of it in the last forty-eight hours. Borchardt and then this bloody, bloody play. You think it's right to allow this kind of play, Sherm? Corrupt the kiddy's morals?'

'Legal or personal opinion?'

'I don't give a damn which!'

'Legally, yes. I don't believe in curtailing any free expression especially not among students.'

'You're a ravening anarchist.'

'Perhaps.'

'No goddamned perhaps about it! Yes!' He poured himself another drink.

'You're drinking too much, Frank. Remember your status.'

'Screw status! I'm just another miserable bastard making his way through this goddamned life!'

'You want a personal opinion?'

'What about?'

'The play . . . this kind of revenge melodrama?'

'Why not?'

'You asked me for it?'

'Is that right?'

'You're really something! How much have you had already?'

'I've had it up to here.' As Torrance was making a cut throat gesture to illustrate what he felt to Markham, Linda entered the room.

She caught his gesture, and, he thought looked contemptuous. She shone with triumph; her face a bright gleam from the cold cream and cold water needed to wash away the make-up. Her eyes were still bright with excitement and the whole room burst into applause when she walked in. 'Bitch,' Torrance mumbled under his breath. 'Bitch.'

Sometime later, the stage manager broke through a crowd of admirers, mostly young men, surrounding Linda and whispered to her that President Torrance wanted to see her in his office at midnight. She looked around for him to acknowledge the meeting but he was nowhere to be seen.

When she turned her attention back to the group surrounding her, it was a half-hearted act. Some of Vittoria Corombona's fear trembled inside her.

Torrance approached Meredith Hall with a sense of event, for all his fear at being found out, he wondered if maybe Columbo hadn't made a mistake and found another person whom he would brand as the killer and thus let the President, himself, off the hook. With the same thought, he also considered bolting, making a run for it, getting out. No dignity in that, however.

Following this line of thought, he strode up the palm-lined path in the dark toward the building, he came to the conclusion that Columbo could never crack the case correctly. Maybe Linda would be brought into it as the Lieutenant hinted, but . . . but chances were she would never implicate Torrance.

Then again . . . ?

With this last doubt he entered the darkened building and climbed the stairs to his office.

No one was there.

He switched the light on. The reception room and his tidy New England workspace were just as he'd left them late this afternoon.

The clock on the mantle read 12.03. He decided to sit down and wait fifteen minutes for Columbo.

He settled into his desk chair. Obviously, he thought, comforted, he couldn't be the target of Columbo's investigation if the Lieutenant wasn't here yet. Columbo must be delayed somewhere seeking that last bit of evidence that would nail his suspect.

A moment later Linda stood in the office door. 'What are you doing here?' Torrance asked, standing up. He was deeply shocked and surprised.

'Mary Jane told me you wanted to see me. I sure as hell didn't want to come.'

'I didn't give any Mary Jane – whoever she is – any such message. Leave right now.'

'If that's true, Frank, forget it. It's too late to leave.'

'No it's not. Go. Go.' He was practically shouting.

She crossed the room and sat serenely on the sofa, crossing her long legs. 'Your greeting was enough. It shows you know me. I'm sure we're being monitored. It's finished.' She shrugged her shoulders. 'Curtain about to come down.'

'I don't know what you're talking about, Miss Kitteredge.'

She laughed outright. 'Oh, Frank! Are you talking for a tape recorder now. Silly man! We've had it. We're finished. This little rendezvous was rigged. Columbo probably figured the whole thing out. I wonder what tipped him off?'

'You're mad. Insane. Crazy.'

'Oh—! Let's see.'

Urgently, he whispered: 'How can you be so calm?'

'I don't know,' she shrugged. 'But . . . it's in my blood. Like Vittoria Corombona. I guess there's a kind of taint there . . . oh . . . nonsense. Maybe I know we can't get away from it forever . . .'

'There's nothing to tip our hand . . .'

'Yes there is, Frank.'

'What . . . just tell me what?'

'You're basically a decent person. It would have eaten away at you. Not immediately, perhaps, but finally . . . eaten you up alive from inside. The funny thing is I didn't and don't give a damn. If I get caught or not, what do I care? Life goes on in jail or out. And if it doesn't go on? That too would be interesting.'

'You're a cold and crazy bitch. I think you should leave, Miss Kitteredge . . .'

'I think we have enough, Mr Torrance . . .' Columbo stood in the door, two patrolmen behind him. 'Miss Kitteredge is right. If you didn't break now, you would sooner or later. She's really the one that worried me. I didn't think she'd be as straightforward as she just was. Thank you.' Linda nodded.

Torrance tried to play the administrator. 'You can't take what you just heard into court.'

Linda ignored Torrance. She wanted to know how Columbo figured it all out.

'Well, I'll tell you Miss Kitteredge. You had me going in circles till the play tonight and then you both came here just now. I had to prove that connection. I guess that's done.'

Linda shot a look at Torrance, who had crumpled into the chair behind his desk. 'Told you! The minute he got us together it was over. Very sneaky, Lieutenant.'

'I want you to know I was impressed with your acting tonight.'

'If I ever get out of jail, maybe you'll give me a reference.'

Torrance sat glowering and then, the explosion: 'How the hell can you be so calm? What kind of a monster are you Linda? You're being arrested for murder . . . you killed someone. Do you have some kind of moral blind spot? I don't understand you any more. Is life just kicks to you? Is that all? Oh God!' He dropped his heavy alcohol-fuzzed head on his hands on the desk.

Linda looked up at Columbo. 'Do you understand why we did it, Lieutenant?'

'Not everything. Not yet. You didn't kill Borchardt for the fun of it? It's not a Manson-type thing?'

'No. Frank needed to be rid of the Dean . . .'

Torrance's head shot up. 'A lot of good it did me. He knew about us Columbo.'

'Yeah. I figured that. I got that from his correspondence and talking to certain people. I wasn't sure it was Miss Kitteredge till tonight. Don't feel bad, Mr Torrance. I kind of knew it was you from the beginning. Miss Kitteredge's presence here didn't give your participation away.'

'How could you know, Lieutenant?'

'Well, sir. It was the resin on your shoes and the make-up on your chin. I couldn't figure out why you were at that theater the night of the murder unless it was to murder Mr Borchardt or arrange it. The make-up . . .'

'What make-up?'

'When you came to the lecture after you killed Mr Borchardt. There was a spot of make-up . . . stage make-up on your chin . . .'

'From Linda . . . ?' he muttered weakly.

'I guessed it must have been one of the girls in the show. And Miss Kitteredge had been the last one in the theater . . .'

'We figured no one could find the motive, Lieutenant.'

'You're the motive Miss Kitteredge. There's not much a man in Mr Torrance's position can do to disgrace himself except get involved with a student or murder someone . . .'

'I did both, Lieutenant. O.K.' He stood up. 'Let's get it over.'

Columbo placed them both under arrest. A squad car waited on the drive in front of Meredith Hall.

Sherman Markham waited next to the squad car. He stopped Torrance and Linda as the two patrol men led them out. 'I thought whoever it was would need a good lawyer. I'm sorry it's you, Frank . . . I hope you'll let me represent you.'

'And Linda too. Sherm.'

'And Linda too.' He agreed sadly.

'Thanks.' The two then entered the police car, which drove away immediately.

'You wonder,' said Columbo, 'why a man like that . . . educated . . . right at the top . . .' He shook his head and thrust his hands into the pockets of his raincoat.

'The flesh and the ego, Lieutenant. They lead a lot of people into some pretty grisly acts.'

'And a pretty girl like that, with talent? You know Professor, I see things on this job I can never really tell my wife about. She . . . she's got this deep admiration for people in the academic and art world. Why she wouldn't believe a bad thing about these people . . . !'

Markham clapped him on the shoulder. 'Don't tell her Columbo. It would shatter her faith.'

'I wouldn't do that sir, not at all.'

'Well, it's been a pleasure seeing you work.'

'Thanks.' Columbo gave a little wave with his hand and disappeared into the darkness leading to the theater where his car was still parked.

Markham stood a while in front of Meredith Hall watching Columbo disappear into the darkness. Tomorrow Meredith College would have to begin the difficult business of finding a new President and Dean.